TORN

←—— THE MISSING: BOOK 4 ——→

TORN

MARGARET PETERSON
HADDIX

SCHOLASTIC INC.
New York Toronto London Auckland
Sydney Mexico City New Delhi Hong Kong

No part of this publication may be reproduced, stored in a retrieval system, or transmitted in any form or by any means, electronic, mechanical, photocopying, recording, or otherwise, without written permission of the publisher. For information regarding permission, write to Simon & Schuster Books for Young Readers, an imprint of Simon & Schuster Children's Publishing Division, 1230 Avenue of the Americas, New York, NY 10020.

ISBN 978-0-545-38644-9

Copyright © 2011 by Margaret Peterson Haddix. All rights reserved. Published by Scholastic Inc., 557 Broadway, New York, NY 10012, by arrangement with Simon & Schuster Books for Young Readers, an imprint of Simon & Schuster Children's Publishing Division. SCHOLASTIC and associated logos are trademarks and/or registered trademarks of Scholastic Inc.

12 11 10 9 8 7 6 5 4 3   12 13 14 15 16/0

Printed in the U.S.A.   23

First Scholastic printing, September 2011

Book design by Tom Daly based on a design by Drew Willis
The text for this book is set in Weiss.

FOR TRACEY

ONE

"We didn't know what we were doing," a voice whispered near Jonah's ear.

Jonah struggled to pay attention. He and his younger sister, Katherine, had just traveled through time, from one foreign era to another. He was becoming an experienced time traveler—a thirteen-year-old expert, you might even say. So he'd learned that when he first landed in a new place and time, he just had to expect his brain to be a little fuzzy.

And his eyes.

And his ears.

And . . . Really, for all Jonah could tell, he and Katherine might be seconds away from being burned at the stake or tortured on a rack or trampled by stamped-ing horses fleeing a war. And he wouldn't be able to see or hear or notice any of those things until it was too late.

Anything was possible now.

No, no, Jonah told himself. *It's* history. *Everyone knows how it's supposed to go. JB wouldn't have sent us here if we were going to be in danger. Not right away, at least.*

JB was the true time-travel expert. It had taken a while, but Jonah trusted JB. The problem was, Jonah didn't have a very high opinion of the past. Twice now he and Katherine had gone back in time with other kids. They'd been sent to fix history and save endangered children. Each time, their mission had gotten a little complicated . . . and endangered *them.*

Jonah could have drowned.

Katherine could have died in battle.

Their friends could have been murdered.

Near misses, Jonah thought. Those two words, together, had more meaning than Jonah could bear to think about at the moment.

And what's supposed to happen now? Jonah wondered. *I don't know anything about what happened in . . .* 1611. He was proud that he could remember the year they'd been sent to. But the pride was followed by a shiver. *What if this is the year that fate catches up with us?*

That word—*fate*—prickled at his brain. It was too much for him to think about right now. He blinked and squinted, trying desperately to bring his vision into focus. A moment ago he'd managed to read a paper held close to his eyes. But beyond that range everything was just a gray fog around him. The only thing he could hear was a muffled *thump-thump, thump-thump*, off in the distance. He could feel some cold, hard surface beneath him—wood, maybe? *Wet* wood? Why would he be lying on wet boards?

"Jonah? Katherine?" The voice spoke again, sounding so tinny and distorted that Jonah could barely understand. Jonah wasn't sure if the problem was his ears or the fact that the person was speaking to them from another time. "We tried. We really tried. . . ."

"JB?" Jonah moaned.

"Who else would it be?" the voice said.

"Maybe . . . Second," Jonah's sister Katherine whimpered nearby. "Second was talking to us on the way here. . . ."

"*Second* was talking to you again?" JB asked, clearly alarmed. "Oh, no. . . ."

Once upon a time—well, once upon a time in the distant future—Second had been JB's most trusted employee. They'd worked together restoring history to its proper course after unethical time travelers had messed it up.

Then Second himself had decided to change the past.

He'd sabotaged Jonah and Katherine's trip to return

their friend Andrea to the year 1600—and to her original identity as Virginia Dare, the first English child born in North America.

Second had set up a reckless scheme to shift time from its intended path—to improve it, he said. He'd manipulated Andrea and Jonah and Katherine and their new friends Brendan and Antonio. He'd risked their lives.

And he'd achieved everything he'd wanted to in 1600.

He'd even managed to break down the barriers protecting time after 1600, so the results of his changes had rippled forward, changing everything along the way. Now all of time—and history itself—was in danger of collapsing, unless Jonah and Katherine could keep 1611 stable.

No pressure, Jonah told himself. *Nothing to worry about.*

It was too overwhelming to think about saving all of time, all of history, all of humanity from the year 1611 on. Jonah focused his thoughts a little more narrowly, on just one person:

Andrea.

Second promised, Jonah thought. *He promised if we fix 1611, we can rescue Andrea. . . .*

Actually, it was a package deal. Second had promised that Jonah and Katherine could rescue Brendan and Antonio and JB as well. *All* of them were stuck in the past. And, sure, Jonah wanted each of his friends to be safe. But it was Andrea he thought about the most: Andrea with her soft gray eyes, her gleaming brown hair, her stubborn hope that . . .

Katherine slugged Jonah in the arm.

"Stop daydreaming about Andrea," she said. "We don't have time for that."

Sheesh, how did she know? Jonah wondered. He stopped himself from looking again at the drawing of Andrea on the paper he was holding in his hand. The drawing was torn from a book that had dropped on him only moments after they'd arrived in 1611, and it proved that Second's changes had arrived too. But it also proved that somewhere back in time Andrea was still okay.

Jonah realized Katherine was waiting for an answer.

"I wasn't daydr—," Jonah started to protest, but Katherine interrupted.

"Yeah, you were," she said. "You're looking all lovesick and gloopy again."

"You mean, the way you look any time you're around Chip?" Jonah taunted. He was trying to think of a better put-down, when something else struck him. He managed to raise himself slightly on trembling arms and turn his head toward his sister. "You can see my face already?" he asked. "You're getting over the timesickness that fast?"

He squinted but could see Katherine only as splashes

of color in the general fuzziness. Was that blur of yellow her hair? Pink, her T-shirt? Blue, her jeans?

It seemed wrong, all those bright colors in the midst of the gray haze.

We don't belong here, Jonah thought, shivering. *Katherine doesn't. I don't.*

Which would make fixing 1611 even harder.

"I—," Katherine began, but stopped, because JB was talking again.

"I see that we made even more mistakes than I thought," JB said.

Now Jonah could tell where JB's voice was coming from: a small metal box that had fallen between him and Katherine. It looked like some antique meant for—what? Jonah wondered. Holding a candle? Scooping flour?

It didn't matter. Jonah knew that the box was anything but antique, and that its appearance was completely fake. If it was transmitting JB's voice, it was actually an Elucidator, a device from the future that could camouflage itself to fit any time period. In Jonah's time—the early twenty-first century—it always looked like an ordinary cell phone.

Having it look so primitive now probably meant that the technology in 1611 would be really, really lame. But Jonah was just glad to *have* an Elucidator. On their trip to 1600, Second had made sure they lost it. They'd been entirely cut off.

And exposed.

Jonah managed to hold himself back from grabbing the Elucidator and clutching it like a little kid with a security blanket. But he did interrupt JB to ask, "Shouldn't we set the Elucidator to make us invisible? Right away?"

Invisibility was one of the Elucidator's best apps.

"Um . . . no," JB said nervously. "Not just yet."

This was odd. Usually JB was all about being cautious, not taking chances. Staying hidden.

"Listen," JB said. "We don't have much time. We really messed up."

"We *know*," Katherine said. "We saw what happened in 1600."

Jonah shivered again, practically trembling. This was odd too—he didn't remember shivering as a symptom of timesickness before.

"That's not what I mean," JB said. "What we thought about time itself—a lot of *that* was wrong. You have to understand—time travel was so young then. We were as confused as all those early European explorers in their Age of Discovery. All their crazy notions . . . Did you know they thought that in the summertime the North

Pole would be as hot as the equator, because of the constant sunshine?"

"So then someone went there, saw the glaciers, and figured out they were wrong," Katherine said impatiently. "Just like you guys went back in time, figured out what it was like, and—"

"No." JB's voice was hard suddenly, almost angry. "We didn't find out that quickly. Time travel is not like geography. There are so many complications. So many extra variables. Things that don't show up until you've made mistake upon mistake upon mistake."

Jonah realized that his vision was clearing. He could see past the Elucidator now, past Katherine. Beyond her a thin layer of ice shone dully on a weathered wood floor and a cluster of equally weathered-looking barrels. And beyond that—Jonah squinted—was fog.

So I still can't see everything, he thought. He snorted, because the salt water in the air was stinging his nostrils. *No, wait—that's real fog! That's why I can't see anything!*

He sat all the way up, swaying only slightly. Now he could see the spot where the wooden floor met a wooden wall of sorts. But the wall rose up only about three or four feet. After that—Jonah looked toward the gray, foggy sky—there was an intricate arrangement of ropes leading up to billows of dingy, tattered white cloth.

Sails, Jonah thought. *Rigging. We're on a ship.*

The ropes also had a sheen of iciness. Icicles hung from the side of the ship.

Jonah finally understood why he couldn't stop shivering: He was wearing only jeans and a T-shirt, and it was absolutely freezing here. The world around them seemed like the kind of place that never thawed.

He gasped.

"Are you sending *us* to the North Pole?" he asked.

TWO

"No, no," JB answered. "This is 1611."

He said the date as if it was supposed to mean something to Jonah and Katherine. When neither of them jumped in with something like, "Oh, yes! Of course! 1611!" he sighed and started to explain.

"By 1611 the early explorers had figured out that sailing over the pole wouldn't work," JB said, sounding like a teacher who really, really wished he were dealing with smarter kids. Or at least more educated ones. "You're in James Bay, in what's going to be Canada. You *are* on Henry Hudson's ship—for a little while longer, anyway—and he was the one who disproved that whole 'warm seas near the North Pole' theory. But you're on a later voyage of his—his last, in fact."

Jonah shivered again at the ominous tone in JB's voice.

He glanced over at Katherine, and she was actually grinning.

"Henry *Hudson?*" she said, sounding almost as excited as if they were talking about one of the Jonas Brothers, not some dusty old explorer. (*Or,* Jonah thought, *some icy old explorer?*) "One of the kids stolen from history was named John Hudson, right?"

"Correct," JB said.

"Same family?" Katherine asked.

"I think you can figure it out," JB said. "John was Henry Hudson's son."

Katherine gave Jonah's shoulder a shove, almost knocking him down.

"So *that's* who Jonah really is!" she practically squealed. "He must be, since you didn't bring back any other missing kids!"

Jonah felt his stomach lurch. He didn't think that he could blame timesickness anymore. Maybe it was seasickness?

He'd known that he was one of the missing kids from history, stolen from time by the unethical kidnappers/ baby smugglers from the future, Gary and Hodge. He'd known that at some point he would have to go back to his original time period, to repair the damage Gary and Hodge had left behind. He knew that he should have asked ages ago exactly who he was, what time period he'd come from.

But it was scary knowing he was supposed to be someone other than Jonah Skidmore, ordinary kid, adopted by an ordinary family.

No, it was terrifying. Jonah's general strategy had been to try not to think about it.

Katherine—who wasn't adopted, who'd never had to worry about being anybody but herself—had no such fears.

She slugged Jonah's shoulder again.

"Way to go, Jonah!" she exclaimed. "Son of a great explorer!"

"You want him to be the son of Henry Hudson?" JB interrupted her rejoicing. "Son of an explorer whom history has accused of being crazy, monomaniacal, or possibly just really, really bad at managing underlings?"

"JB," Katherine said in a low voice, as if she were trying not to let Jonah hear. "You really shouldn't say things like that if we're talking about Jonah's biological father."

"Fortunately, we're not," JB said drily. "Jonah is not John Hudson."

Jonah felt a wave of relief. Suddenly his stomach felt fine. Just . . . hungry.

He remembered that back in 1600 they'd eaten nothing but fish. Jonah had never been a big fan of fish, mainly because he could eat a bunch of it and be hungry again fifteen minutes later.

Time travel kind of threw things off, but Jonah really did feel as if it'd been eleven years since he'd had anything to eat.

"Crazy, monomani—whatever. Who cares?" Jonah said. "What I want to know is, does Henry Hudson have lots and lots of food on his ship?"

JB gave a low chuckle.

"Ah, his story could have turned out so much differently if he did," JB said.

"Please!" Jonah begged. "Can't we have some food before we do whatever we're supposed to do here? I'm starving!"

"Sorry, but no," JB muttered. It was hard to tell with his voice just coming from the Elucidator, but Jonah had the sense that JB was looking guiltily side to side, glancing back over his shoulder. His voice varied that much in volume.

"Couldn't you just yank us out of time, let us eat, then bring us back?" Katherine asked. Usually she made fun of Jonah for being hungry all the time—if she was asking too, things must really be bad. "Or let us have something we can eat fast, without making any noise? We won't leave any crumbs, we promi—"

"No!" JB exploded. "I can't! We don't even have time to *talk* about food right now! Everything's about to start!"

Jonah's stomach started churning again. But it wasn't just the hunger. There was something about the way JB sounded—as if he was even more scared than Jonah and Katherine. And was it Jonah's imagination, or was there just the faintest hint of a siren sounding through the Elucidator along with JB's voice?

"*What's* about to start?" Jonah challenged. "You have to tell us—"

"We're out of time," JB said tensely. "There! Do you see the tracer?"

A ghostly figure appeared on a narrow stairway from below the deck. It glowed faintly, throwing its eerie light into the fog around it.

Jonah knew that this wasn't actually a ghost, just like the Elucidator wasn't actually an antique metal box. Long ago, on their first trip through time, Jonah had learned about tracers, the mostly see-through figures that represented what people would have done—how time would have flowed—if time travelers hadn't intervened. Only time travelers could see them; they didn't really exist.

Jonah still thought tracers were creepy. His experiences in the year 1600 had made him even more suspicious of them. He watched this one warily.

"Is it just that one tracer, coming up those stairs?" Katherine asked in a barely audible whisper. "Or are there any real people behind him? Do we need to hide?"

"Don't worry about that yet," JB whispered back.

The tracer walked unsteadily to the side of the ship. It was hard to tell anything about the tracer's identity, because he was wrapped in a ragged, dirty cloak. Then the tracer leaned out over the railing. The wind knocked back the hood of his cloak, revealing a filthy tangle of light-brown hair and a bony, pockmarked face.

"Allow me to introduce John Hudson," JB muttered. "Ship's boy for his father's last four voyages."

"That's a *kid*?" Jonah asked. "His face is so shriveled up I thought he was an old man."

"That's from frostbite, scurvy, knife fights . . . It's been a rough winter," JB said grimly. "And spring."

The tracer of John Hudson turned away from the railing and yelled back toward the trapdoor.

"Ice is breaking up!"

It took Jonah a moment to realize that the hoarse, creaky voice didn't come from the tracer's mouth—even though his lips moved in perfect sync with the words.

Instead the voice came from the Elucidator.

"JB?" Jonah asked. "What are you doing? Whatever happened to not changing time? And—"

"I'm not changing time. I'm trying to keep time on track." The voice coming from the Elucidator sounded like JB again, though a very hushed, tense version. "The rest of John Hudson's shipmates are supposed to hear the boy yell out about the ice breaking up. Since no one can hear a tracer, I had to do it for him."

Jonah squinted at the Elucidator. His brain still wasn't working at its usual speed, but something seemed odd about JB's answer.

"Why didn't you just bring the real John Hudson back a few moments ago and let him say it himself?" Katherine asked. "Wouldn't that be easier?"

"Yes, it would," JB said, and now it sounded as if he was talking through gritted teeth. "That's how we would have preferred to do it."

"Then why didn't you?" Jonah asked, catching up. "What's the problem?"

"That's one of the things I've been trying to tell you," JB said.

"*What?*" Katherine asked, sounding exasperated.

JB paused. Jonah was almost eerily aware of the seconds ticking by—seconds marked off by the ship bobbing up and down in the water; the icicles dripping on the deck; the wind blowing the raveling end of a rope back and forth, like a pendulum. Time was not waiting for JB's answer.

"I've been trying to tell you," JB finally said, "that we lost the real John Hudson."

THREE

"*Lost!*" Jonah exploded. "You mean, like, he died?"

"Oh, no," JB replied. "At least, he hasn't yet."

"I know, I know!" Katherine said. "Is it like that old movie—what was it called? *Back to the Future?*—where time travel almost made it so this kid and his brother and sister were never born? Did some time traveler before 1611 make it so John Hudson never existed?" Katherine clapped her hand over her mouth and turned about two shades paler than her natural color. "Did *we* do that in 1600?" Now she clutched her brother's arm. "Oh, Jonah, I hope that doesn't happen to you!"

Thanks a lot, Katherine, Jonah thought. *You're really helping here.*

"Calm down!" JB commanded. "That's not what happened. First of all—John Hudson was already born *before* 1600. He's a teenager, can't you tell?"

"Oh, yeah," Katherine said, a little sheepishly.

"I'm sure the real John Hudson is absolutely fine, not in any danger of being extinguished from history," JB assured her. "It's just, we had a little . . . uh . . . technical difficulty getting him back here in time."

Jonah watched the tracer, hunched again at the railing. Now he really did seem like a ghost, some empty husk of a boy who might as well have died.

With all the time-travel worries Jonah had tried to avoid thinking about, he'd never once thought to worry about it being impossible to get someone back to his native time.

What if that happened with Jonah and whatever time period he was supposed to belong in?

Does this mean that John Hudson doesn't really belong here after all? Does this mean that JB might be wrong about . . . everything?

Jonah's head was starting to hurt.

Katherine slammed her hand down on the deck. She was already jumping to another question.

"So what are you going to do?" she asked accusingly.

"Oh, we've figured out a plan that ought to work," JB said faintly.

"What is it?" Katherine asked.

Back home Katherine had been agonizing over whether, the next year in seventh grade, she would try out for cheerleading or basketball. She'd made it sound like the decision of a lifetime, the chance to choose her true identity: Was she a girly girl or a jock?

Now Jonah saw that she already had a true identity. He could see her future very clearly: She was going to grow up and be a prosecuting attorney. She already sounded like one.

And JB was answering her questions. He was answering meekly, almost humbly, as if Katherine deserved to have the upper hand.

"Let me explain," JB said. "See, Gary and Hodge were just a little premature snatching John Hudson out of time. They were so sloppy." The scorn in his voice was palpable. "If they'd just waited a few hours, they could have pulled John Hudson out with no problem, no possible chance of damaging time."

"So why didn't they?" Jonah asked, curious in spite of himself.

"Because it's a lot easier for time travelers to land on the deck of a seventeenth-century, three-masted sailing ship—rather than in a tiny rowboat bobbing among the ice floes," JB said contemptuously. "Especially if they're lazy."

"Oh," Jonah said. He could understand wanting to take the lazy way out.

"So John Hudson is supposed to end up in a rowboat?" Katherine asked. "In *ice?*"

"There's a mutiny afoot," JB said. "We're just seconds away . . ."

A crash sounded below the deck. The tracer version of John Hudson straightened up and rushed over to the stairs. He peeked over the edge, then slid down the icy steps.

Silence.

"Is the real John Hudson supposed to be doing something down there?" Jonah asked.

"No, no, just hiding," JB said. "Watching. Waiting. Until . . ."

"But he's not really there!" Katherine said, sounding panicked. "He's not going to end up in any rowboat! What's going to happen then?"

Katherine's panic was contagious. Jonah started thinking about all the awful things that could happen if John Hudson missed some crucial moment in his life: *time ruined forever . . . me never getting to eat again . . . Andrea and the others stuck in the past forever . . . Oh, Andrea . . .*

"Don't worry!" JB said sharply. "John Hudson doesn't actually have to *be* in the rowboat. His shipmates just have to *think* he is!"

"Well, what's going to make them think that if you can't get the real John Hudson back?" Katherine asked.

"Our brilliant backup plan," JB said. "Jonah's going to play John Hudson's part."

FOUR

For a moment even Katherine was stunned into silence.

Jonah thought about how John Hudson's tracer had looked: the wild, uncombed thatch of hair; the hollow, scarred cheeks; the sunken eyes; the missing teeth. Granted, Jonah hadn't looked in a mirror in a while. But he didn't think he looked like that.

"Um, I'm not a very good actor," Jonah said, because if nobody else had noticed that Jonah didn't look anything like the grotesque John Hudson, Jonah would feel really stupid trying to point that out. "And I wouldn't know what to say or do."

It wouldn't be like in the past time periods they'd visited, where their friends had joined with their tracers and instantly known everything the tracers were thinking, and how to act. People could mesh only with their own tracers.

"It's not really a matter of *acting*," JB said. "You're just being a space filler. A prop. All you have to do is stay in the general vicinity of the tracer when he comes back up the stairs. This situation coming up—it's all about Henry Hudson. Not his son."

"Hold on," Katherine said. "You said there's a *mutiny* about to happen? What if someone shoots Jonah? Or stabs him to death?"

Jonah hadn't thought of that. He stopped worrying that he might look as hideous as John Hudson.

"Let's just say his costume will be both bulletproof and stabproof," JB said. "Even his wig and mask."

Oh—a costume, Jonah thought. *Wig. Mask. Of course.*

"I'm game," Jonah said, immensely cheered at finding out that he would only have to pretend to be wild-haired, frostbitten, pockmarked, gap-toothed and disgustingly scarred.

"Are you *crazy*?" Katherine asked. Jonah couldn't tell if she was aiming her question at him or JB.

But the words weren't even out of Katherine's mouth before Jonah felt something rough and scratchy settle over his shoulders. He looked down at what appeared to be an exact replica of the black cloak John Hudson's tracer had been wearing. *Or not an exact replica*, Jonah told himself. *Not if this one's bulletproof.* His face felt oddly stiff, and when he reached his hand up to touch it, he discovered craters and crooked scar lines. One seemed to be lightly oozing blood.

"Jonah?" Katherine whispered. Her eyes were wide with horror. "Is that really you in there?"

"Sure," Jonah said, but even his voice came out sounding as if it belonged to John Hudson.

"We embedded voice modification software in the teeth overlays," JB explained. "Pretty amazing, isn't it?"

Jonah ran his tongue over his teeth—which suddenly seemed chipped and broken-off and crooked, as if he'd just gone through some kind of reverse orthodontia. He gagged, and choked back nausea. Even though it fit loosely, the woolen coat suddenly felt as if it were suffocating him. He tugged at his face, at his hair, trying to pull off the mask and wig. They didn't budge.

Jonah couldn't breathe. He whipped his body from side to side, struggling to escape.

"Katherine—slap him!" JB ordered. "He's going into hysterics!"

"I'm not going to slap him!" Katherine snapped. "Not when he's in agony like that!" She threw her arms around his shoulders. "Oh, Jonah, I know you're in there! Don't worry—we'll get you out! I love you! You're the best brother ever!"

This was so ridiculously sappy that Jonah couldn't help himself: He started laughing.

Maybe that was all he needed, because when he stopped laughing, he found he could breathe fine.

"Can I keep this costume when we go home?" he asked JB. It was still weird to hear his voice come out sounding like somebody else's, but he was able to hold the panic at bay. For now. "This would be great for Halloween! Look how easy it was to scare Katherine!"

He lifted his arms in a zombie/Frankenstein/monster-type move: "Argghh!"

Katherine shoved him away.

"You are so mean!" she said. "I was really worried about you! I thought you were actually scared."

"Not me," Jonah bragged, even though it was a lie. "Nothing scares me."

"Would you two *focus?*" JB asked. "The tracer's going to be coming up the stairs again in a moment. With other people, *real* people—"

"Then you have to make Katherine invisible," Jonah demanded. He might tease Katherine like crazy, but he wasn't going to leave her exposed in plain sight in the midst of a mutiny.

"I'm *trying*," JB said grimly.

"What do you mean, trying?" Jonah asked.

Then, in the next instant, Katherine became as transparent as a tracer. Jonah had seen his sister—and himself and others—turn invisible before. But it was still bizarre to watch. He knew that anyone from 1611 would be able to look right through Katherine; the ship's crew wouldn't know she was there. Only Jonah, as a time traveler, was able to see her faint outline.

To him it looked like she'd turned into glass.

"What about the Elucidator?" Katherine asked, since it was still sitting on the deck, in plain sight.

"Oh, um, right," JB said, sounding distracted.

For a moment the Elucidator seemed to quiver, but it never quite turned invisible.

"I can't do it," JB said. "Jonah, quick—put it in your pocket—"

Can't do it? Jonah thought. *Can't?* First they'd lost John Hudson, now the Elucidator's invisibility was failing—what else could go wrong?

There wasn't time to ask. Jonah snatched up the Elucidator and tucked it and the picture of Andrea inside his cloak. Just then the dim glow of John Hudson's tracer appeared at the top of the stairs. The tracer walked purposefully to a door beyond where Jonah and Katherine were sitting. He lifted his hand as if he were about to knock.

"Should I go stand there and knock?" Jonah asked. "If I'm playing his role . . ."

He was already standing up. But that was as far as he got. It was hard to keep his balance on the rolling deck. And he had another moment of fear: What if he did knock? What if someone answered the door? What was Jonah supposed to do then?

"Go stand over there, but whatever you do, don't knock!" JB whispered tensely. "The tracer's going to chicken out."

Indeed the tracer had frozen, his hand poised by the door. Then he backed away.

Jonah noticed that the tracer's lips were moving.

"What'd he just say?" Jonah asked.

"He said, 'He never likes to hear bad news. And I'm not sure . . . ,'" JB whispered back.

"Should you say that for him? Should I?" Jonah asked.

"No, no—nobody could hear him, so it doesn't matter what he says," JB whispered.

Like that whole 'if a tree falls in a forest . . .' question, Jonah thought. *If no one hears him, who cares if there's a sound or not?*

Jonah was feeling light-headed, and still wasn't entirely certain that his thoughts were making sense. Was it from the timesickness? The panic? The effort of trying to figure out what he should do as John Hudson?

He stepped carefully into the space that John

Hudson's tracer occupied. Crazily Katherine stepped up right behind him, as if they both needed to stay within the tracer's dimensions.

Or maybe she was scared too.

A strangled cry sounded behind them, and both of them whirled around. A man's head was just dipping down out of sight at the top of the stairs.

Jonah had no clue what the tracer was thinking— Jonah had no idea what to think himself. Had the man slipped on the icy stairs? Had someone attacked him?

The tracer began creeping toward the stairs, stealthily, as if he wanted to see what had happened to the man but didn't want anyone to see him. Jonah shuffled forward too, not quite getting the rhythm of the tracer's steps.

Oh, yeah, you kind of have to wait between rolls of the ship. Is the water always this rough? Jonah wondered, lurching forward, catching his balance, then lurching forward again.

Jonah reached the edge of the stairs only a split second behind the tracer. He peeked down into the—what would it be called? The hold? But he couldn't really see what had happened, because his eyes hadn't adjusted to the darkness below. He squinted, trying to make out shapes.

Then he heard screaming above him.

"No! You are not going to hit my brother! Jonah! Watch out!"

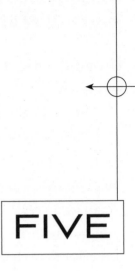

FIVE

Jonah whipped his head around to see a giant club descending toward him. It was already too close to dodge, but Jonah tried anyway. He hunched his shoulders and brought his arms up to protect his head and rolled to the right and . . .

And how is it that that club hasn't hit me yet?

He realized that he'd squeezed his eyes shut, defensively, but now, still rolling, he dared to open one eye partway.

The club was still poised above him, but he was no longer directly in its path. He scooted a little farther to the right. The club still hovered overhead.

It wasn't moving.

"What the . . . ," Jonah muttered.

He pulled himself together enough to sit up and look

toward the handle end of the club. A cruel-faced sailor was holding on to it with filthy, infected-looking hands.

The sailor wasn't moving either.

Looking around—more leisurely now—Jonah realized that John Hudson's tracer was frozen in place as well, sprawled across the deck in the exact spot where Jonah had been only seconds before. The tracer seemed completely unaware of the man above him. And his head was directly below the club, the perfect target.

The tracer wasn't moving at all, not even with the rolling of the ship.

For that matter the ship wasn't rolling anymore, either. It was also frozen in place, at the peak of a swell lifting its right side up and plunging its left side down.

"So, JB," Jonah said, calmly taking the Elucidator out of his cloak. "Why'd you decide to freeze time?"

"I've got to stop Katherine from screaming over every little thing," JB complained from the Elucidator. "Or else—"

"Little?" Katherine shrieked, darting out from behind the club-wielding sailor. "Jonah, that man was going to kill you!"

Jonah saw that she'd been tugging on the sailor's arms, trying to hold them back.

"Bulletproof! Stabproof!" Katherine sputtered. She

grabbed the Elucidator out of her brother's hands and yelled directly at it. "You made it sound like Jonah was going to be safe! How's a lousy costume supposed to protect him against being clubbed to death?"

"Katherine," JB said. "Jonah. Look at the man holding that club."

Jonah looked.

The only thing Jonah had noticed before was the filth and the cruel expression. Now he studied the sailor's face: the eyes even more sunken than the tracer's, the cheeks pitted with sores, the cheekbones and chin jutting out sharply, as though they could break right through the papery skin.

"I've seen skeletons in better health," JB said. "He can barely even lift that club."

It was true: Even frozen in place, the man's arms looked as though they'd been trembling with the exertion of holding the club in the air.

"He couldn't have really hurt Jonah," JB said. "But John Hudson—the tracer—he isn't in very good shape himself. One little tap, and he would have been out of the action until he's on the rowboat."

"So I'm supposed to go through a whole mutiny pretending to be unconscious?" Jonah asked. Sure, he'd been worried about what he was supposed to do and say. But wasn't this a little . . . insulting? "Couldn't you just have used a dummy to play this role, and left me out of it?"

"Wouldn't have worked," JB said, the tension back in his voice. "There wasn't time; we didn't have enough control. . . ." Jonah felt an icy blast of air, and the ship lurched slightly to the left, before locking into position again, still seriously tilted. "Hurry! I can only hold this for so long! Jonah, get back into place!"

Jonah shot a glance at his sister. Generally Jonah was a pretty obedient kid. Life was easier that way, he thought. Spend two minutes taking the trash out to the curb, and then you didn't have to listen to a forty-five minute lecture about how "everyone in the family has responsibilities; everyone has to pull his own weight" and "Jonah, we're just trying to prepare you for adulthood, when you'll have to take care of yourself and other people too. . . ." And on and on and on.

But Jonah had also always been around grown-ups— parents, teachers, coaches—who were big on explaining everything. "The reason you have to clean your room is . . ." "You have to show all your work on that math problem because . . ." "If you pass the ball instead of trying to take the shot on goal yourself, then . . ."

Jonah wanted to yank Katherine aside—was there a way to doubly pull someone out of time? He wanted to be able to confer with her privately, somewhere JB couldn't hear them. What if obeying JB was a really, really bad idea? What if they couldn't trust JB after all? What if he was lying? Should Jonah and Katherine be staging a mutiny of their own?

Jonah tried to convey all of those questions in one quick glance. He didn't know if Katherine understood any of them, but she scrunched up her face into an agonized expression.

Then she shoved the Elucidator back into his cloak and muttered, "Go ahead. I'll watch out for you."

Jonah thought about throwing back a sarcastic comment like, *You and what army? You're barely five feet tall! And do you even weigh eighty-five pounds?* But really, she probably was strong enough to overpower the skeletal sailor.

Cautiously, Jonah lay down on the deck, awkwardly trying to fit his body into the space occupied by the tracer. At the last minute he turned his head back, defiantly. Maybe he was stupid enough to let himself be hit in the head by a club, but he wasn't going to do it blindly.

Wham!

The club slammed into Jonah's forehead. Jonah reeled back.

Okay, maybe the sailor wasn't strong enough to swing that very hard himself, Jonah thought. *But . . . gravity! Wasn't*

anybody thinking about how gravity would pull the club down?
That was a hard hit!

Automatically Jonah lifted his hand to his head, to rub the sore spot.

"Jonah, you had better pretend you conked out, just like the tracer, or else he'll hit you again," JB whispered, very, very softly.

Jonah dropped his hand and let his body go limp.

"Jonah!" Jonah heard Katherine wail, as she flung herself down to crouch over him.

The sailor who'd hit Jonah had to have heard her too.

"Witchcraft? Bedevilment?" he muttered in a frightened voice.

Jonah opened one eye just a crack, just enough to see the sailor looking side to side, his eyes bulging in terror.

"Katherine, shut up! Jonah's fine! He's just acting, the way he's supposed to," JB hissed, again so softly that Jonah was fairly sure the sound couldn't travel up to the sailor's ears.

Jonah couldn't see what Katherine was doing, but the sailor shrugged, as if deciding he had other things to worry about than devils and witches.

"I found the pup," the sailor called down into the hold. "I gave 'im what was coming for 'im, I did."

As far as Jonah could tell, nobody answered. But the

sailor began tugging on Jonah's legs, pulling him toward the side of the ship.

If he lifts me up like he's about to toss me overboard, I am not lying still for that, Jonah thought. *I don't care what JB wants me to do.*

It was hard enough lying still while being dragged. The sheen of ice on the rough deck probably made Jonah's body slide more smoothly, but it stung the bare skin of his face.

So much for the protective mask, Jonah thought. He didn't want to think the next thought, but it came anyway: *What if there isn't a protective mask? What if it's just ordinary makeup?*

The sailor stopped tugging on Jonah's feet—now he was wrapping a rough rope around Jonah's ankles, looping the rope around Jonah's wrists, and tying all of them together. Then he shoved Jonah's body into the dim area behind a row of barrels.

"And that's where you'll stay," the sailor muttered. "Cur!"

A big watery blob hit Jonah's cheek.

One huge droplet from a melting icicle? Jonah wondered. Spray splashing in from the sea?

"Jonah!" Katherine's urgent whisper sounded right beside Jonah's ear. "That man just spit on you!"

"Eww, sick!" Jonah barely remembered that he had to whisper, barely remembered to open his eye halfway and make sure that the sailor had turned away before Jonah brought his hand up to his face and rubbed away the spittle. Because his wrists and ankles were tied together, he had to jerk his feet up at the same time.

"Loosen the rope, will you?" he asked Katherine. "Just in case . . ."

Katherine bent near him, picking at the knots.

"Ow—broke a fingernail," she muttered, with an exaggerated pout.

"You'll *live*," Jonah muttered back.

"Shh!" JB hissed at both of them. "Don't change anything!"

Katherine paused for a second, glared down at the spot in Jonah's cloak where he'd tucked the Elucidator, and then went back to picking at the knots.

"Nobody's going to know," she muttered. "And this way, we'll be able to protect ourselves if we have to."

She pulled the end of the rope back. Jonah spread his wrists and ankles apart, making room to slip the ropes off if he had to.

Footsteps sounded on the other side of the barrels, and Jonah shut his eyes and let his head loll back, just in case.

"Okay, they went on past," Katherine whispered.

"There's a group of them, going up to that door where the tracer was afraid to knock . . ."

She fell silent.

"What's happening now?"

"They're trying to decide who's going to knock—wait, I think one of them just volunteered. . . ." She drew in a sharp breath. "No, they're going to fight about it."

It was maddening, lying there waiting for Katherine's descriptions. Jonah sat up—his head woozy and throbbing—and peeked around the side of the barrel.

The fight seemed to be happening in slow motion. One man shoved another; a third man drew back his fist to punch the first. But the potential puncher seemed to have balance problems—just the action of moving his fist was enough to topple him over backward. He landed with a *thunk* on the deck and lay there blinking up at the sky, as if wondering what hit him.

Jonah choked back laughter.

"Jonah, shh, they'll hear you," Katherine hissed. "And get down, before someone sees you! The door's opening."

Jonah crouched down but kept his head up, watching.

The handful of sailors who hadn't ended up flat on the ground were standing back from the door. They twisted their hands; they glanced nervously at one another.

The man closest to the door pulled out a gun.

"Um, JB?" Katherine whispered. "I know you said Jonah's safe because his costume is bulletproof, but what about me? If that man shoots his gun over in this direction—"

"He's not going to," JB whispered back.

"Maybe you should crouch down behind the barrel a little more," Jonah whispered.

Katherine hunkered down, almost on top of Jonah. Both of them peered around the barrel.

The door had swung all the way open now. A man stood in the doorway, calmly regarding the gun.

"So it's come to this," he said.

Jonah could see the gun shaking in the other man's hand.

"M-master, you leave us no choice," he said. "To avoid an icy grave we must sail for home now, whilst we can, whilst it still be summer."

Summer? Jonah thought. *This is summer?*

"JB, are you sure we aren't at the North Pole?" he muttered.

JB didn't answer.

Neither did the "master" in the doorway.

"Bind his hands!" the man with the gun cried.

Two of the other sailors stepped forward with ropes.

The man standing in the doorway held his wrists out, as if he didn't care what the others did.

"So the glory of discovery will be mine alone," he said. "Long after you are dead and forgotten, people will praise my name as they sail the Hudson Passage!"

Katherine drove her elbow into Jonah's back.

"That must be Henry Hudson!" she whispered.

"I'm not an idiot!" Jonah whispered back. He really wanted to ask, *Is there a Hudson Passage somewhere? Is he right?* But, well, he didn't want to look like an idiot.

"Won't be no 'Hudson Passage,'" the man with the gun said. "We're sailing for home."

"'C-cause, you just want to drive us all to our deaths, looking for something that isn't there," one of the other men said.

He looked around at his buddies for agreement.

They nodded, and shuffled forward menacingly.

Hudson didn't step back.

"You've lost your faith," he said. "Now? Just when I've found out—" He broke off, and stared coldly out at the assembled men. "No, no, it's not worth discussing with the faithless."

Jonah couldn't help being impressed that Hudson seemed so calm. Either he was crazy or really, really brave.

Or maybe he's blind? Jonah thought. *Doesn't he see that gun?*

The man with the gun lowered it.

"How could you have found out anything?" he asked. "We've been trapped in the ice since Monday. Trapped in ice in *June!*"

"I am a brilliant sea captain," Hudson said airily. "I read the winds. I read the waves. I see things no other man could."

Now the other men looked at each other nervously. Some in the back—the ones who'd fallen on the deck— were whispering together.

The man with the gun glared at the whisperers, then aimed the gun more precisely at Hudson.

"Do you see that you're not the captain anymore?" he asked.

Hudson looked directly at him for the first time.

"I see that you will hang for mutiny," he said. "You, and anyone who joins you."

This set off more whispering.

"We'll say you died a natural death," the man with the gun said. "We'll swear an oath together—nobody will speak the word *mutiny*. Nobody will ever know."

Hudson's head shot up.

"You'll say you left me in the shallop," he said. "At my request."

"*Shallop?*" Jonah whispered. "What's that?"

"It's the rowboat," JB whispered back."Or—kind of like one."

"He's *asking* to be put out in a rowboat?" Jonah asked. "In ice?"

"It beats being shot," Katherine said in a shaky voice.

"Would you deny an old sea captain his last wish?" Hudson pressed.

Now the man with the gun stepped back to whisper with the others.

Jonah caught bits and pieces of the argument, because the sailors weren't very good at keeping their voices low.

"But what if *we* need the shallop to go out fishing?" one sailor moaned.

"Will this make us more or less likely to hang?" another yelped.

Finally the man with the gun stepped back toward Hudson.

"Fine," he said. "You get the shallop. And any man crazy enough to follow you." He nudged Hudson's chest with the gun. "We get to keep the food you've been hiding."

"Wait—there's not going to be any food in the rowboat, either?" Jonah asked.

"Jonah—shh!" JB hissed.

"Go get the others," the man with the gun muttered to the sailors beside him. Two broke off from the group and scurried down the stairs—Jonah had to admire the way they could walk so quickly even on the rolling ship.

A few minutes later the men reappeared, carrying or prodding along a small group of even more sick-looking sailors.

"Are those *corpses?*" Katherine asked. "Are they going to send Hudson out in a rowboat with a bunch of dead bodies?"

"No, they're not dead . . . yet," JB whispered grimly. "Just very, very close. Hudson's going to be out in a rowboat in the ice with a bunch of dying sailors."

Katherine sank down to the floor, sliding away from Jonah. She wasn't trying to peek around the barrels anymore. She stared unseeingly at the dark wood of the cask before her.

"I don't get it," she said. "Okay, sure, the sailors are mad at Henry Hudson because they're ready to go home and he's not. But those other guys are already dying. You don't put dying people out in a rowboat in ice. You tuck them into bed and feed them, I don't know, chicken noodle soup."

"When no one's seen a chicken since they left England more than a year ago?" JB asked her. "When every bite that crosses a dying man's lips is food that the others can't have? When every man on this ship is already scared he's going to starve to death?"

Jonah shivered. He wasn't sure if it was because of the cold or because JB's words were so harsh. This ship was an awful place. It would be cold and brutal and nasty even if they weren't floating through ice.

Jonah poked at John Hudson's unconscious tracer.

"Hey, dude," he whispered. "Don't you want to wake up and be a hero? Fight back for your dad and all those dying sailors?"

But of course Jonah's hand slipped right through the tracer.

Katherine turned her head toward her brother.

"Jonah?" she said. "Do you think—"

She broke off, because the sailors were screaming on the other side of the barrel now.

"Watch out!"

"No, no, don't—"

"He's got a sword!"

SIX

Jonah sprang up to watch.

"Stay out of sight!" JB ordered.

"Oh, sorry," Jonah muttered, crouching slightly so his eyes would barely show above the top of the barrel. He expected JB to complain about that, too, but the Elucidator was silent.

Jonah eagerly turned his gaze toward Henry Hudson. Hudson had been talking a few moments ago about being an old sea captain, but maybe that was just a bluff. Maybe he was really youthful and athletic and agile—and good with a sword. Maybe he'd had one hidden in his sleeve. He could have used it to slash the ropes binding his wrists, then flicked the tip of the sword against the gun, swinging it out of the other man's grasp. Stuff like that happened all the time in the movies. Jonah hoped he'd sprung up in time to see some really fancy moves, like Henry Hudson spinning the gun around the tip of the sword a few times before flinging it out into the water.

But Henry Hudson was still standing quietly by the door, his wrists still tightly bound.

Only the man with the gun had moved. Rather than pointing the gun at Henry Hudson, he'd turned it, so he was now aiming at . . .

Jonah had to crane his neck and try to look around the mast.

A whole cluster of sailors was jumping around over by the stairs. Jonah saw a flash of sword, but he couldn't tell who was holding it. One of the sailors on the edge turned around and yelled at the man with the gun.

"Don't shoot! Don't shoot! You'll hit one of us!"

"Then stand back!" the man with the gun yelled.

"But he's chasing us!"

The cluster of men scattered and re-formed, as the man with the sword lunged toward the others, and the others lunged toward him, trying to knock the sword out of his hands. This was nothing like a sword fight in a movie: The swordsman was clumsy and awkward, and the men around him were panicky and stupid, moving in a pack when they should have divided up.

Jonah remembered that he'd seen much better swordsmanship in the fifteenth century, at the Battle of Bosworth.

He'd also seen swordsmen die.

He closed his eyes.

"Doesn't he know he's going to get shot?" Katherine fumed. "It's like a game of rock-paper-scissors—guns beat swords, every time."

"Not necessarily," JB said softly. "Guns weren't very accurate in 1611."

"So that guy is afraid to shoot?" Katherine asked. "Afraid he'll hit one of his friends?"

Jonah opened his eyes just a crack, to see that Katherine was pointing toward the man with the gun. Jonah followed her gesture—and then stared.

"Look at that!" he muttered.

Henry Hudson had stepped forward and put his hand against the gun—not to grab it, but to push it aside.

"My loyal mate, John King," he called out.

Jonah craned his neck again to see across the deck. The man with the sword glanced up.

"Yes, Captain?" he said.

"Put down the sword," Hudson said. "Come with me in the shallop, and we shall meet our glory away from these cowards."

The swordsman, John King, stopped parrying and thrusting, but he kept a hold on the sword.

"By 'meet our glory,' you don't mean dying, do you?" King asked suspiciously.

"No, no," Hudson said, waving aside the question, as if death weren't even a possibility. "I'm talking about the Northwest Passage. I know how to find it now."

Northwest Passage? Jonah thought. He had a vague memory of talking about that in some social studies class. *I would have paid a lot more attention if somebody had told me I was going to end up on Henry Hudson's ship in Canada. Or what's going to be Canada someday.*

The sailors reacted as if Hudson had said he knew how to win the lottery, guaranteed. Some looked awed. Others were shaking their heads, rolling their eyes.

"He lies!" the man with the gun yelled. "Just like he's lied all along! Do you want to spend another winter here? Do you want this to be your grave?"

He pointed out into fog, toward the dark water.

Even the sailors who'd looked amazed began to grumble and complain.

Like almost everyone else John King was watching Hudson and the man with the gun. One of the nearby sailors kicked King's hand, sending the sword scuttling across the deck.

One of the other sailors instantly grabbed King's arms and pinned them behind his back.

King struggled, then slumped helplessly when he couldn't break the other sailor's grip.

"To the shallop!" Hudson cried, raising his arm in the air. He fixed the man with the gun with a withering gaze. "You do not need to coerce me. I go of my own free will."

Hudson marched forward, the others trailing him a bit uncertainly.

"If this is a mutiny, why does it seem like Henry Hudson is still in control?" Katherine whispered.

"In control?" Jonah whispered back. "He's going to end up in a rowboat and his enemies are going to get the ship! With all the food!"

"But it seems like that's what he wants," Katherine said.

"Reverse psychology," JB muttered. "He's really good at it. Especially for someone who's so bad at interpersonal relationships. Unless . . . Oh, no! *No!* It can't be!"

"What?" Jonah and Katherine said together.

JB didn't answer.

"JB?" Jonah said.

Still no answer.

On the other side of the ship Henry Hudson and John King were climbing into a small boat—the shallop. The mutineers were lifting the dying sailors in behind them. Probably someone would come looking for John Hudson in a few moments, to carry him to the shallop as well.

Jonah didn't relish the thought of getting into a rowboat in icy water, but the sooner that happened, the sooner he could be done with 1611. *The sooner I can rescue Andrea. And get something to eat*, Jonah thought, grinning slightly. He looked down, thinking that JB would probably want him to make sure he mimicked the position of John Hudson's tracer exactly.

But the tracer wasn't glowing anymore. Jonah squinted, trying to make out the form of a tracer in the dim light sifting through the fog. Hadn't the tracer been right there a moment ago?

He was, Jonah thought, horror creeping over him. *But he isn't anymore.*

The tracer had completely vanished.

SEVEN

"Um, uh, JB?" Jonah stammered. "Uh . . ."

He racked his brain—could he somehow have missed seeing the tracer get up and walk away? He looked over toward the group of men by the shallop, but no tracer stood among them. What if John Hudson's tracer had awakened and slipped over the side of the railing? He could right now be swinging hand over hand around the outside of the ship, getting ready to spring out to attack the mutineers and rescue his father after all.

But wouldn't JB have mentioned that Jonah was going to have to do that?

"So, JB, if I'm supposed to be acting like John Hudson, where should I be right now?" Jonah asked, trying to sound casual.

"I don't know!" JB snapped.

"'Cause, see, I kind of lost the tracer," Jonah admitted.

"So did I!" JB said. "We lost all the tracers! Every . . . single . . . one!"

Jonah tried to get his brain around that. No tracers meant there was nothing to show how history was supposed to go. There were no guidelines now. No help.

"Isn't that a good thing?" Katherine asked. "The tracers only show up if time travelers change something. So if there aren't any tracers, that must mean everything's back on track. So—can we go home now? Or back to 1600 to make sure everything's okay there, too?"

"Everything is not back on track!" JB fumed. "Everything is completely messed up! It's so messed up we don't even know what's wrong!"

Jonah had never heard JB sound like this before. Even back in 1600, when everything had changed, JB had stayed fairly calm. He'd focused on getting the kids safely away from the disaster.

"So—do you need to just pull us out of this time period?" Jonah asked, trying to sound casual.

"I *can't*!" JB said. "Time travel doesn't work anymore! Time itself doesn't work anymore!"

"Don't say things like that," Katherine mumbled. "You're scaring me."

"But it's true!" JB said.

Jonah knew it wasn't his imagination this time: There were definitely alarm bells and sirens going off in the background, behind JB's voice.

"You can still talk to us," Jonah said. "Katherine's still invisible. I still sound like John Hudson—I bet I look like him too, right, Katherine?"

Katherine nodded. But she was biting her bottom lip.

"So a lot of things are still working," Jonah said. "Right?"

"Do you know how close we are to . . . not . . . ," JB began, and it was clear that he was speaking through gritted teeth. "It's like the two of you are right on the edge of a cliff, teetering on the brink. . . ."

"Really not helping, JB," Katherine said.

Jonah thought that if she weren't already invisible, her face would probably have turned very pale. And then in the next instant she *was* pale. She didn't look like glass anymore; she looked like the tracing paper they'd used in art class back in elementary school—kind of see-through, but definitely there.

Jonah reached up and yanked on Katherine's arm, pulling her down below the level of the top of the barrel.

"Ow!" she complained, shoving away from him. "What'd you do that for?"

Then she stopped pushing. When Jonah looked back,

she was holding her hand up in front of her face, examining it as if she'd never seen it before.

"Ohhh," she moaned.

And then in the next instant she was invisible again.

"Sorry about that," JB said through the Elucidator, but his voice was tinny and faraway. "Things may be . . . in and out . . . for a while. . . . Try . . . keep . . . like John . . ."

The Elucidator went silent.

"Does this mean we just fell off the cliff?" Katherine muttered.

"You're invisible again," Jonah said, trying to think of something comforting. "And I haven't stopped looking like John Hudson, have I? So we've got two out of the three things we need. Two out of three—that's, like, sixty-six percent. That's a passing grade in school."

But was time like school? And, now that he thought about it, did he really want to keep looking like John Hudson? So far all that had done for him was that he'd gotten hit over the head and dragged behind some barrels.

"We're stranded!" Katherine said. "We're going to be stuck in 1611 forever!"

"No, we're not," Jonah said. "We stay here long enough, eventually it will be 1612." He grinned, trying to make it into a joke. "Those guys said it was June already. We've just got six months to go to a whole new year."

"We stay here six months, we're dead," Katherine said bitterly. "Starvation, remember?" She pointed out toward the sailors. "It's not like they have any food to share."

Oh, yeah, Jonah thought. *Food.*

His stomach churned anxiously. He'd been hungry at various points during his previous trips through time, particularly in 1600, when they'd had nothing to eat but fish. But there'd actually been plenty of fish, a virtual all-you-can-catch, all-you-can-eat buffet.

Fishing around ice chunks probably didn't work very well.

We could starve, Jonah thought. *We really could. Or freeze to death. Or . . .*

Katherine's eyes, in her still-invisible face, were large and round and terrified. Her bottom lip trembled.

"Hey," Jonah said. "Hey! Stop that! We'll be fine! The only thing we don't have anymore is JB telling us what to do. We got along without him when we lost the Elucidator in 1600, right? And when we hit the mute button in 1483? We survived those years, we can survive this!"

"Those years are over," Katherine said. "We know how they turned out. Well, mostly," she added.

"JB said to stay like John," Jonah said. "I bet if I just keep acting like John Hudson, that will help time. And it's not brain surgery! All I have to do is act like I'm knocked out."

He waited for Katherine to make a crack like, *Yeah, acting brain-dead, even you should be able to handle that.*

When she didn't say anything, he peeked around the side of the barrel.

"See, I bet there's someone coming for me right n—" He froze on the word "now" as soon as he saw what was going on at the other side of the deck.

Nobody was coming to get John Hudson, to put him in the shallop. Nobody was going to.

Because the mutineers were already lowering the shallop over the side of the ship, down toward the icy water.

EIGHT

"They're leaving without me?" Jonah said incredulously.

He sat bolt upright, his foot jerking out and striking the bottom of the barrel.

The barrel seemed to move in slow motion, its top section wobbling back toward Jonah and the railing. Jonah reached up and shoved at the rim, trying to maneuver it back into position.

The shove would have worked perfectly—if Jonah had been on flat, unmoving dry land. But his shove came just as the ship hit a swell, dipping down and then up.

The barrel crashed forward, slamming against the deck. It began to roll toward the mutineers.

"I'll get it! Lie still!" Katherine hissed.

It was the hardest thing in the world to slump over and pretend to be unconscious, when he had so much adrenaline coursing through his body. Every nerve ending he had seemed to be yelling, *No! Do something! Run!*

Jonah let one eye drift halfway open—sometimes people did that when they were unconscious, right?

He immediately wished that he'd kept his eyes closed.

On the other side of the deck the mutineers had whirled around. They looked perplexed at the sight of the barrel rolling toward them. They looked even more perplexed when the barrel came to a complete stop, even as the deck tilted further to the side.

The lead mutineer whipped out his gun.

He pointed it right at the barrel—which meant it was pointed toward Katherine, since she was the one invisibly holding the barrel back.

"What evil is this?" the mutineer muttered. "Does a spirit possess our water cask?"

"Proof that our master was dabbling in devilment!" one of the other mutineers cried out.

"Nay—'tis proof that your mutiny is evil!" yelled back one of the men in the shallop.

And then they all just stood there. It made Jonah feel as if he were watching a defective DVD, the kind that leaped forward or froze at random. Time hadn't stopped—the ship was still lurching up and down, jerkily; the shallop, on ropes, swayed unevenly back and forth. The men weren't completely motionless either. The man with the gun had begun to squint, as though trying to center his aim more precisely . . . more precisely in Katherine's direction.

I know you said Jonah's safe because his costume is bulletproof, but what about me? Katherine had asked JB, only a few moments ago.

JB hadn't told Katherine she was safe.

"Oh, hey!" Jonah said, jumping up. The loose ropes fell from his wrists and ankles. "Like my new barrel trick?"

He took a few steps forward, past the ropes. He whispered, "Get out of the way!" in Katherine's ear, and then hopped up to stand on the side of the barrel. He thought maybe he could walk it forward and back like some circus performer, and then the sailors would be so mesmerized that they'd forget how strangely the barrel had stopped.

But evidently being a circus performer took a lot of training and practice. Jonah didn't even manage to stand completely upright before he came crashing down, slamming his chin against the side of the barrel. He landed in a heap on the deck, and the barrel rolled on, crookedly, until it cracked against the railing.

Water gurgled out, pooling on the deck.

Jonah sincerely hoped their water wasn't in as short supply as their food.

"Oops," he said. "Sorry."

Everyone was staring at him now. They seemed beyond baffled. The sailor who'd bashed Jonah over the head and dragged him over behind the barrels looked as if he'd forgotten all about Jonah. Maybe the man was just stunned to see "John Hudson" reappear, fully conscious and acting ridiculous.

But Jonah couldn't quite understand the other men's expressions.

What if JB was completely wrong about what was supposed to happen to John Hudson? What if he was never supposed to end up in the shallop—what if he was supposed to sail away with the mutineers, leaving his father behind in the ice?

Jonah looked toward Henry Hudson, as if he would provide some kind of clue. Maybe Hudson would be gazing at him proudly and lovingly, and muttering, "My son, you know I'd never leave you behind." Or maybe he would look disappointed, if he'd been hoping that his son could stay safely on the ship and manage to get back to England, even with a pack of double-crossing mutineers.

Instead Henry Hudson looked more baffled than anyone else.

"They sent you back?" he murmured, disbelievingly. "They sent you back?"

He seemed devastated at the sight of his son. Indeed

for the first time he began acting like a sea captain being kicked off his own ship in disgrace. His shoulders slumped and his face fell. His head pitched forward; he brought his bound hands up to his mouth, as if he needed to hold in his cries of outrage, just for dignity's sake.

Hudson's quite visible despair seemed to help the mutineers make up their minds about what they should do next.

"Think ye that the shallop needs its own ship's boy?" one of the sailors called out.

"Aye," another replied. "He'll be shallop's boy now!"

Jonah had never heard the word *shallop* until a few minutes ago, but he could tell this was supposed to be a huge insult, maybe like Lance Armstrong being forced to ride a tricycle. Some of the sailors laughed so hard they fell down on the deck.

"Devil's spawn should stay with the devil!" one of the men cried.

He advanced toward Jonah, scooped him up, and then thrust him into the partly lowered shallop.

Oddly, as soon as Jonah landed in the boat, everyone else shifted positions. It wasn't a matter of making room for him, because there was plenty of room. It was more as if, once he was there, everyone else could fit into their proper spots, where they belonged.

"Good job," someone whispered, the ghost of a voice.

It seemed to be coming from Jonah's cloak.

The Elucidator? Jonah wondered. *JB?*

He wanted so badly to yell out, *Okay, did that fix everything now? Are we back on track?* But he was only about a foot away from the nearest sailor, and it would be impossible to converse with his own cloak without being noticed. He looked around for Katherine, thinking maybe she'd have some good suggestion about what to do.

But of course nobody had scooped up Katherine and tossed her into the shallop.

Katherine was still back on the ship.

NINE

Katherine was standing by the railing, a few steps apart from the mutineers. Her mostly see-through face was twisted in anguish. As soon as Jonah looked her way, she began exaggeratedly mouthing words. Jonah wouldn't have said that he was very good at reading lips—especially mostly invisible lips—but he could tell what she was trying to say: *What should I do? What should I do?*

She pointed down at the ship, and lifted her other hand questioningly, then pointed to herself and out toward the lowering shallop. Her sign language was clear too: *Should I stay on the ship? Or should I try to climb into the shallop?* Now she lifted both hands, palms open to the sky, and grimaced. This meant, *How could I possibly get into the shallop now?*

With all the mutineers clustered near the railing, Katherine wouldn't be able to reach the shallop without knocking a few of them out of her way. Anyhow, the shallop was being lowered on ropes, and it was far enough down that Katherine couldn't jump in without knocking everything off-kilter.

Jonah could imagine Katherine trying to climb down one of the ropes, throwing the entire shallop off balance and pitching everyone—Jonah, Henry Hudson, John King, and five sick, dying sailors—into the icy water below.

"Don't!" he said out loud. "You can't!"

Who cared what the sailors around him thought he meant?

Katherine's face twisted even more. Jonah didn't need lip-reading or sign language to know what she was thinking: *It's bad enough to be stranded in 1611, expecting to starve to death, but to be stranded* alone?

"You've got a better chance of surviving on the ship," Jonah said, and this was meant as a parting gift to his sister, his best effort at a hopeful good-bye. He wasn't sure if this was true or not. Sure, all the food was on the ship. And sure, Katherine was invisible, so she could sneak around eating whatever she wanted. But those mutineers seemed a little nutso—and they had weapons—and what if Katherine lost her invisibility again?

Jonah wondered if he should toss the Elucidator up to Katherine, so at least she'd have that, if it worked again.

But how could he do that without everyone noticing?

Jonah had been staring so intently at his sister that he'd mostly ignored everything going on around her. But now he let his gaze slide over to the men clustered along the railing. One man in particular was watching Jonah very carefully. As soon as his eyes met Jonah's, the man called out, "Aye, lad, I know you are only trying to protect me. But I know who I trust the most on water."

The man evidently thought Jonah had been talking to *him*.

Jonah wanted to say, *No, no, I'm talking to my sister. Who you can't see because she's invisible*—or something that would sound a little more reasonable, but would convince the man that Jonah had nothing to do with him. But the man had already turned to the head mutineer.

"If ye must do this, then put me into the shallop too," the man said.

"What? Staffe, have you lost your mind?" the head mutineer said. "You've disagreed with the master near as much as the rest of us! He's punished you for nothing—nothing!"

"But I'd trust Henry Hudson in a shallop to sail me out of here before I'd trust the rest of you to navigate this ship," the man—Staffe?—said. "Let me take my tools and I'll go."

"But the master doesn't want to sail out of here," some of the other mutineers mocked. "He's just going to sail around in circles looking for the Northwest Passage."

Jonah really did wish he could remember what that was. This time the men said the words as scornfully as they might say "fairyland" or "Shangri-la"—someplace nice but completely imaginary.

"Still," Staffe said, setting his jaw firmly. "I'm going. In a mutiny doesn't every man make his own choice?"

There was grumbling around him, but the men operating the pulleys began raising the shallop again.

Now it was Jonah's turn to mouth words at Katherine: *You come too! When he climbs into the shallop, you worm your way in too!*

And she mouthed back, grinning, *I know! I will! Don't worry!*

Staffe stood waiting at the railing while someone went back for his "tools"—whatever that meant. It turned out it was a wooden box. When Staffe turned around to take the box, Katherine brushed past him. Staffe startled slightly; maybe Katherine's ponytail had slapped against his cheek. But he didn't say anything, only straightened up and looked around, a baffled expression on his face.

"Go, then, if you're leaving," the lead mutineer said brusquely.

By then Katherine had scrambled into the boat. She hugged Jonah, doing her best to keep away from the sailors around them. Jonah thought that the last time he'd willingly let his sister hug him, he'd been about six years old. But there was something comforting about huddling together, even as the shallop dropped lower and lower.

They landed with enough force that icy water splashed up into the boat. Only a little of it hit Jonah and Katherine, but it was enough to make Katherine start shivering violently. Jonah didn't care how strange he would look: He spread out his cloak so it draped over Katherine, too.

"Thanks," she whispered. "That helps."

Fortunately, everyone else in the boat was distracted, watching the man who'd wielded the sword—John King?—maneuvering a rope so that they were still tied onto the bigger ship.

"They'll let us back on as soon as they search for food," one of the skeletal sailors croaked in a raspy voice that sounded as if it took his last ounce of energy. Or maybe just his last ounce of hope. "Won't they?"

Nobody answered. By craning his neck and looking up, Jonah could tell that some of the sailors on the larger ship were unfurling the sails.

But we're still attached, with the rope, Jonah thought. *They can't sail away from us.*

Just then someone from the larger ship bent down and slashed a knife through the rope. The end fell into the water, causing another icy splash. And then the ship sailed away into the fog.

"We're adrift!" one of the sailors sitting near Jonah cried. "We're all going to die!"

The despair in his voice was horrible, like a tidal wave washing over everyone. Jonah felt his own hopes begin to ebb away.

No, no, he thought. *This is what has to happen. What happened in original time. It's terrible if everyone cast out into the shallop dies, but . . . this means that once we're out of sight of the ship, I can stop acting like John Hudson. Our job will be done. JB can pull us out of 1611 and everything will be okay. For us, anyway. And Andrea and Brendan and Antonio . . .*

Katherine gasped beside him.

Jonah scowled at her. How could she draw such attention to herself? Then he realized that many of the others in the shallop had gasped as well. He turned, and saw what they were all so upset about.

A huge chunk of ice was floating right toward them. Now that Jonah was down on the same level as all the ice, he could see how massive the ice chunks were. They were practically icebergs. Even the ship probably would have been damaged if such a big ice chunk hit it.

But in the shallop . . .

We're going to sink, Jonah thought. *This is the end.*

"JB!" he screamed. "Get us out of here! Now!"

TEN

Jonah kept his eyes wide open, eager for his first glimpse of a nice, safe, sterile time hollow or—better yet—his own home back in the twenty-first century. But the desolate, foggy view around him didn't change, except that the ice slid closer and closer and closer. . . .

JB wasn't going to rescue them. Maybe he couldn't.

"Raise *our* sails!" Henry Hudson screamed. "Row toward starboard!"

Jonah felt a hand slam against the side of his head.

"I said, row!" Henry Hudson growled.

It was Katherine who thrust the handle of an oar into Jonah's hand. Jonah glanced around and saw that John King, on the other side of the shallop, was already dipping an oar of his own into the water. And Henry Hudson and the man the others had called Staffe were setting up sails in the middle of the boat.

So a shallop isn't just a rowboat, Jonah thought numbly. *It can use sails, too. . . .*

Katherine was already helping him pull on the oar, coordinating with John King's paddling. But it was the sails that really saved them. As soon as the wind caught the first billow of cloth, the shallop lurched to the right, narrowly edging past the towering ice.

Jonah slumped against the side of the shallop in relief.

"I *am* an excellent captain!" Henry Hudson screamed out into the fog. "You had no right to banish me!"

Just in the moment that they'd spent dodging the ice, the larger ship had vanished completely. Henry Hudson's screams echoed off the ice around them.

Banish me . . .

Banish me . . .

A hand slammed against the side of Jonah's head once more, trapping air painfully against his ear.

Okay, I'm guessing that John Hudson and his dear old dad didn't have the best relationship, Jonah thought, cringing away from the man.

"Who's this JB you were calling out to?" Henry Hudson asked suspiciously. "Some code name? Could it be? My own son plotting against me?"

"No, no," Staffe said smoothly, holding on to the sails.

"He was merely being reverent. He said, 'JC.' Jesus Christ. Your son was beseeching the Lord for our aid. And where do you think these winds came from? His prayers were answered!"

The wind in the sails was pulling them away from the ice at an amazing speed.

Henry Hudson gazed suspiciously back and forth between Jonah and Staffe. As soon as Hudson turned his head, Staffe winked at Jonah. Then he straightened out his face into an innocent gaze as soon as Hudson's eyes were upon him again.

So that's how it works, Jonah thought. *Captain Hudson's mean to his son—er, me, for right now—but this Staffe guy protects him. . . .*

It wasn't as good as JB protecting him by yanking him and Katherine out of time, but Jonah was glad not to be hit again.

"Sir?" John King asked, taking over the sails from Staffe. "Shall we sail toward shore, to set up camp at the winter cabin?"

Toward shore? Winter cabin? What's he talking about? Jonah wondered. He remembered what JB had said earlier, that the men from Hudson's ship had had a rough winter and spring. Evidently they hadn't stayed on the ship all that time. They'd packed up to get away from the floating ice and the howling winds and camped out on shore.

Jonah stared at the ice floating past the shallop and reminded himself that it was June now. Summertime. If this was what June was like, he *really* didn't want to see what it'd be like to live through January and February here.

"The winter cabin?" Hudson sneered. "Odd's bones, man, we're sailors, not rabbits. At least, *I* am. Henry Hudson does not cower in a hole when there are treasure routes to be found, glory to be attained . . ."

He's crazy, Jonah thought. *Totally bonkers. Has he already forgotten that he's been thrown off his own ship in disgrace? That we're in a glorified rowboat? In ice? Shouldn't he be more concerned about staying alive than anything else?*

"But if we go to the cabin, we can lay in supplies for next winter," Staffe said, taking up John King's argument. "By next spring a rescue expedition is bound to come for us—"

"Henry Hudson will not be *rescued!*" Hudson thundered, smacking his hand down on the side of the shallop in his fury. "Henry Hudson will sail home in glory, with a shipload of treasures from the Orient!"

"The Orient"? Jonah thought. Wasn't that one of those old-fashioned expressions his grandparents used sometimes? *Would it mean the same thing in 1611 that it means to Grandma and Grandpa?* he wondered.

It couldn't. Grandma and Grandpa talked as if the Orient was China and Japan and other places in Asia.

We're somewhere in Canada right now. Does Henry Hudson really think we're going to sail this shallop all the way to China or Japan? And then back to England? Jonah didn't know much about geography, but that had to be a long way. Like, halfway around the world and back again. *Hudson couldn't go that far even if he still had the ship! Could he?*

"You still believe in the Northwest Passage?" one of the sickly, dying sailors murmured. He sounded as if those might be his last words. "Even now?"

There were those words again: "Northwest Passage." Some old memory stirred at the back of Jonah's mind. Something from fifth-grade social studies, something Mrs. Rorshas had droned on and on and on about, with her talent for making even the most interesting subjects boring. Explorers . . . China . . . treasure . . . What kind of treasure was everyone looking for?

"You shall refer to it as the Hudson Passage, henceforth," Hudson said haughtily. "Because I *shall* discover it."

You've got to give this guy credit for having confidence, Jonah thought. *But how does he think he's going to discover anything in a rowboat—er, sailboat? In ice? How does he think anyone here is going to survive?*

The cloak and mask and wig of Jonah's disguise

seemed too tight again. It seemed harder and harder to draw enough of the cold air into his lungs.

The Northwest Passage, Henry Hudson being crazy, these people who are going to freeze or starve—I can't do anything about any of it, Jonah told himself. *Really, it already happened. It's* done. *JB just has to get me and Katherine out of here. . . .*

Jonah twisted around to the side, pretending he was only trying to block the wind. He hunched over, bringing his face closer to the pocket where he'd tucked the Elucidator.

"JB!" he whispered. "You really could come for us now! I could pretend to fall over into the water or something."

But would one of the others try to jump in and rescue him? Would Staffe? Would Henry Hudson himself?

"Maybe we *should* go to the winter cabin," Jonah said aloud, so everyone in the shallop could hear him. If they landed on the shore, he could sneak away without endangering anybody.

A fist slammed into his jaw; a hand pinned his chest back against the side of the shallop. If Katherine hadn't been beside him, holding him up, he would have fallen over sideways.

"You dare to challenge my authority?" Henry Hudson snarled, looming over Jonah. "I said we will *not* retreat to the winter cabin. We sail on to glory! Do you not remember who is captain here?"

Jonah stared into Hudson's eyes. He felt so odd suddenly, feeling the choices before him. He could say, *Don't you remember you just got kicked out of being a captain? Kicked out of your own ship?* He could say, *Maybe I think it's time you let someone else take over as captain. Since you're not doing such a great job.*

Or he could back down.

Which choice would protect his face from getting punched again?

Which choice would John Hudson have made?

What was the right thing to do?

Normally Jonah made decisions fast, by the seat of his pants. A split second was a long time for him to mull over anything. But whole minutes seemed to be flowing by, and his brain just felt more paralyzed.

Is it always like this, when people don't make decisions right away? Jonah wondered. *Does the decision always get harder and harder, the longer you spend not deciding?*

He could feel the entire boatload of sailors watching him, waiting to see what he was going to do. Even Katherine was waiting, her face twisted in confusion.

What? Katherine isn't going to try to tell me what to do? Jonah thought.

For perhaps the first time in his life he wished she would.

Something hovered at the edge of Jonah's vision, off in the distance. At first Jonah thought it was some remnant of his timesickness problems. An illusion. But there really did seem to be a large shadow sliding toward them through the fog. Was it another ice chunk? How could an ice chunk rise so high above the water?

Jonah squinted, turning his head right and left. He forgot he'd been trying to make a decision.

What I'm thinking can't be right, he thought. *The direction's all wrong. Isn't it?*

The shadow broke through the fog, its shape finally distinct: three masts, billowy sails, a weathered hull. Jonah gasped, unable to believe his eyes.

Everyone else turned and stared with him.

"The ship! It's come back for us!" Hudson cried.

ELEVEN

"Huzzah! Huzzah! Hooray!"

Even the sailors who appeared to be nearly dead found the energy to cheer. They raised weak fists in the air and made feeble attempts at pumping their arms up and down. Toothless grins split across wizened faces.

"I planned this," Hudson said. "I knew it would work out this way. The mutineers were lost without me. . . ."

"Then how could they figure out how to sail back around and come get us?" Jonah muttered.

He looked at Katherine, trying to ask with his eyes: *Does any of this make sense to you? This can't be right!*

She just kept shaking her head, bafflement written all over her face.

The sailor beside Jonah was huddled over a small box, and Jonah realized for the first time what it was: a compass.

Jonah caught a glimpse of the needle jerking around, pointing north.

That's the direction the ship was going, when it sailed away from us. North . . . maybe northeast, Jonah thought. We went west, trying to get away from the ice floe. So now the ship is sailing back toward us from the southwest? Impossible! How could it have circled around us that quickly?

"I'm . . . turned around," the sailor holding the compass muttered. "The directions . . . all off . . ."

"Wydowse, the sickness confuses you," Hudson said, almost kindly. "You're an excellent navigator—you will be again, once you're well."

"The *Discovery* sailed that way," Wydowse said, pointing north. "And now, to come back around from the south . . ."

"Thou knowest this bay has devilish winds and currents," Hudson said, a light tone in his voice, as if he was only humoring the man. "Have faith—we can overcome them!"

"But what if this is a trick?" Wydowse said stubbornly. "Mayhap they return only to torture us further?"

Oh, great—thanks! Jonah thought. Just what I need—more awful possibilities to think about!

Now the boatload of men fell silent, watching the *Discovery* approach.

"Captain! My captain!" a voice called out.

"Abacuk Prickett?" Hudson called back. "Is that you?"

"Aye, Captain," the voice called back. "Everything worked just as we planned."

Planned? Jonah thought.

He could have sworn he saw a flicker of confusion cross Hudson's face too, but the captain covered it quickly, shouting back, "Quite so! Most excellent!"

Hudson began giving commands to angle the shallop toward the ship. Jonah took up his oar quickly, before the man could hit him again.

Most of the men in this boat are too sick and out of it to know what's going on, Jonah thought. *But does Staffe think there's something weird going on? Does John King?*

It was hard to tell. Both men were concentrating on lining the shallop up with the ship, attaching the ropes. The lines began to jerk upward.

"Steady," Hudson called. "Steady does it."

Moments later everyone who could was stepping back onto the deck of the ship. Jonah helped Staffe lift out the men who were too weak to move.

"My captain," a man said, bowing low in greeting.

The man had dirty, unkempt hair, and his clothes were every bit as ragged as the other sailors'. His face was just as pockmarked and scarred. But there was something different about him—an air of strength and confidence that no one else had, not even Hudson himself.

"Was that guy here before?" Jonah whispered to Katherine. "What was *he* doing during the mutiny?"

Katherine shrugged and whispered back, "Never saw him before."

"Prickett," John King said, sounding astonished. "I thought you were lamed. I haven't seen you out of your bunk in days."

Prickett looked toward Henry Hudson.

"It was a plot the captain and I conjured up," Prickett said. "When we heard there was talk of mutiny, he knew he'd need a spy on the inside. Someone who seemed harmless. Not even able to walk! When in reality"—he smiled, in a way that seemed like a threat— "I could win a race with any man here, were it necessary."

"And what did you do with the mutineers?" Hudson asked. "Did you . . . did you carry out my orders?"

Jonah was certain, suddenly, that Hudson had given Prickett no orders. Hudson was as confused by Prickett as everyone else.

"Of course, sir," Prickett said, bowing again. "The other men and I—the ones still loyal to you, who were only pretending otherwise—we put the mutineers out on the ice."

"Juet," Hudson said, looking around. "Wilson. Greene. Pearce."

Jonah realized the captain was listing off mutineers, the ones who were missing now.

"On the *ice*?" Staffe asked. "Do you not feel the air? It's a warming day today. Ice could melt completely by noon."

"Then the water'll be warm enough the mutineers can swim to shore," Prickett said lightly. "They've got better odds than being tried for mutiny back in London, no?"

"Mutineers always hang," Hudson said. He looked around again, this time seeming to make a point of catching each sailor's eye. "Even if it's the captain's word against the entire crew."

Jonah had to hold back a shiver when Hudson looked his way.

He's warning everyone, Jonah thought. *Not to even think about disagreeing with him again.*

"Juet, Wilson, Greene—*they* were leaving *us* to starve," John King said. "Why shouldn't we leave them to drown? Why would we share any of our precious food with such . . . such maggots?"

One of the sickly sailors from the shallop attempted a cheer: "Hear! Hear!" But his voice was hoarse and painful to listen to.

Nobody else joined in.

"The mutineers were hoarding food," Prickett said. "We found it after we put them off the ship. Symmes?"

He gestured, and one of the men behind him—er, no, just a boy—leaned a barrel forward and pried off the lid. Jonah caught a glimpse of rounds of moldy cheese, domes of moldy bread, and greenish-colored . . . meats? Was that what meat looked like when it was thoroughly rotten?

Beside him Katherine gagged silently. She put her hands over her mouth, holding back the retching.

Jonah would have done the same if he'd been invisible. As it was, he clenched his teeth together and tried to think about something besides mold and rot.

Never mind eating, he told himself. *That fish we had back in 1600? Had to be packed with nutrients—enough to last decades!*

Around him the sailors were gasping and cheering and even drooling, as if they'd just seen a gourmet feast unveiled before their eyes.

"Well," Hudson said, his harsh voice cutting through the cheers. "Perhaps there shall be room for extra rations at the noonday meal. *If* everyone attends to their morning work. We've wasted enough time over this treachery. We've business at hand. Wydowse, set a course due west. Everyone—to your stations!"

The men began to scatter.

Oh, no, Jonah thought. *John Hudson was ship's boy—he would have had duties too. Responsibilities. What am I supposed to do?*

Symmes, the boy who'd pried open the barrel of food, drove a pointy elbow into Jonah's ribs.

"You've got lookout," he taunted.

"L-lookout?" Jonah repeated, casting a puzzled glance toward Katherine.

Her jaw dropped. Her eyes got big.

"Oh, yeah," Symmes said. "No trying to get out of it. *I'm* not climbing up there today!"

He pointed one bony finger straight up toward the sky.

Jonah tilted his head back and looked up . . . and up . . . and up.

A wooden tub stood near the top of the tallest mast, practically up in the clouds.

It was the crow's nest.

"I . . . can't," Jonah said. "Not today."

Symmes smashed his foot down on Jonah's, and then twisted it to make it hurt worse.

"Aye, and wouldn't *that* be mutiny?" Symmes asked. "A ship's boy refusing to go up to the top?" He pressed down harder on Jonah's foot. Now the pain shot all the way up Jonah's leg. "Don't think I wouldn't tell."

No, no, Jonah wanted to say. *I believe you! You'd tell! You'd climb up and push me out of the crow's nest if you thought that would help you!*

"I'm going! I'm going!" Jonah said.

He reached for a rope.

TWELVE

Somehow Jonah suspected that the real John Hudson would have reached the crow's nest much faster.

I'm not afraid of heights, Jonah told himself as he inched upward, stopped, then forced himself to keep going. *Not. Afraid. Not.*

For most of his life that would have been true. But last summer at Boy Scout camp there'd been a moment at the top of the climbing wall. . . . Jonah had completely lost his footing. He'd been wearing a climbing harness, of course, so he'd had barely a second of free fall before the ropes stopped him from plunging to the ground. He'd never been in any actual danger. But apparently one second of free fall was all it took to rewire his brain, to switch off the confident voice in his head that had always whispered, *Heights? No problem! Bring 'em on!* And turn on something in its place that sent out whispers of dread: *No, no, don't go up there! You'll fall! You'll get hurt. Maybe even killed!*

Maybe traveling through time and seeing people die for real and knowing that people's lives depended on him—maybe that had something to do with his fear too.

I'm not even wearing a climbing harness, Jonah thought, his muscles locking in place for the umpteenth time.

He glanced down, hoping that someone—Henry Hudson, perhaps? John Hudson's own father?—would call up to him, "Now, now, didn't you forget something? Safety first, remember?" He wouldn't expect anything fancy in the way of safety harnesses—carabiner clips probably hadn't been invented yet in 1611. But wasn't there a spare rope somewhere he could tie around his waist, just in case?

Down on the deck some of the sailors were walking across the still-icy wood with bare feet. A man who must be the cook was hacking away at the greenish meat with a cleaver that barely missed hitting his fingers. A man working with him had an open flame going under a pot of boiling water that threatened to roll away with every swell of the waves.

Okay, "safety first"—not such a big concept in 1611, Jonah thought.

"It's better if you don't look down," a voice whispered below him.

Jonah squinted—it was Katherine. He could barely make out her outline on the ropes beneath him in the wisps of fog.

"What are you doing up here?" Jonah asked. "*You* don't have to risk your life pretending to be John Hudson."

"You think I'm going to stay down there all by myself?" Katherine asked. "Those people are scary."

Scarier than climbing up to the crow's nest? Jonah wanted to ask.

But, of course, *Katherine* wasn't afraid of heights.

"Besides, maybe if we're up there, we can reach JB on the Elucidator," Katherine said. "Maybe, I don't know, it's like a cell phone. They work better if you're higher up."

"No, they work better if you're close to a cell phone tower," Jonah said.

"Well, isn't the mast tall enough to be one?" Katherine asked.

This was illogical in so many ways that Jonah started working out a list in his head.

The Elucidator isn't a cell phone. We don't know anything about how it works.

JB is eleven years away, trapped in 1600. Being at the top of a mast isn't going to move us any closer to him in the past.

It doesn't matter how tall the mast is. If it doesn't have a cell phone tower at the top, it isn't a cell phone tower.

Or an Elucidator tower.

Or . . .

With each item he figured out, Jonah moved his hands and legs up higher on the rungs.

"Though, maybe the mast really isn't that tall," Katherine said. "Remember how time travel can throw off your sense of distance?"

"Of course it's tall!" Jonah said. "It's a mast of a huge ship!"

He looked down again. They were so high up now that the *Discovery* didn't look huge anymore. It looked tiny beneath them—like a toy bobbing up and down in the endless, open bay.

Jonah felt dizzy. Dizzy and terrified.

"I told you. Stop. Looking. Down," Katherine said.

"Stop bossing me around!" Jonah said, fighting the dizziness. Just to prove he didn't need Katherine bossing him around, he reached up again, even as he glared down at his sister.

He saw the faintest trace of a smile cross her face—a smile she hid immediately.

"Are you trying to make me mad?" he asked suspiciously.

"Yep," Katherine admitted. "To distract you from being scared."

Of course that made him madder.

"I'm not scared!" he insisted. And to prove it, he scrambled up the last few rungs of rope, flopped over on his belly, and landed on a circle of canvas-covered wood surrounded by short wooden walls.

He'd reached the crow's nest.

Moments later Katherine gingerly climbed in after him.

"Jonah," she said softly, panting a little, and holding on to the mast that shot up through the middle of the crow's nest. "I'm scared too. It's crazy climbing up here without a harness or net or anything. Mom and Dad would kill us if they knew what we just did."

"That would save us from killing ourselves when we try to climb down," Jonah muttered.

Katherine seemed to turn even paler. Which was amazing, given that she was already translucent.

"Oh, no! I didn't think about how much worse it's going to be climbing down!" she moaned. "Maybe . . . maybe JB will find the real John Hudson and get him in here before his lookout time is over. So *he'll* have to climb down, not us."

She leaned toward Jonah's cloak and pulled out the Elucidator.

"JB! JB, please! Answer us!" she cried into it.

Silence.

"JB?" Katherine whispered.

Nothing.

"He's not going to answer," Jonah said. "Can't you feel how off everything is? How we keep getting further and further from how time is supposed to go?"

He thought about pointing out how long it had been since they'd seen the last tracer, how long the real John Hudson had been missing. But all that just made him feel even more panicked.

Katherine blinked at him.

"Still," she said stubbornly. "None of that should stop JB from talking to us." She held the Elucidator even closer to her mouth and screamed into it: "JB!"

Her voice seemed to echo off the empty sky.

"Shh," Jonah said. "Or else we'll have Henry Hudson up here beating me up again, because he thinks I'm trying to send coded messages to his enemies."

He quickly peeked over the edge of the crow's nest—looking down made him dizzy all over again. But at least no one was staring up at him.

"Do you think Henry Hudson was that crazy in original time?" Katherine said.

"I don't know anything about Henry Hudson in original time," Jonah said sulkily.

"Sure you do," Katherine said. "Remember the Hudson River? And the Hudson Bay? He must have discovered those."

"Congratulations," Jonah said sarcastically. "You just beat me in Geography Bee."

Katherine went on as if he hadn't said anything.

"And JB told us Hudson was supposed to end up in the shallop with his son and a bunch of dying sailors," she said.

Jonah hit his fist against the mast.

"*End*," he said. "The shallop was supposed to be the end of the Hudsons' story. Henry's *and* John's. There's our proof—the ship *wasn't* supposed to come back."

"Why did it? Why's everyone acting so weird? Why won't JB answer us? And what are we supposed to do now?" Katherine asked.

Leave it to Katherine to start adding up everything they didn't know. Jonah would have been happy to leave all those questions unspoken.

No—wait. He could actually answer one of them.

"I guess I just have to keep acting like John Hudson," he muttered. He gazed out at the gray fog, the gray sky, the gray sea. It was hard to see where one ended and the other began. "What do you think I'm supposed to do as lookout? What am I looking out *for*?"

"Icebergs, like in *Titanic*?" Katherine suggested.

Wonderful. That made him feel so much better.

"Since you're invisible, why don't you go back down and eavesdrop on Hudson and Prickett and the others, and figure out what's really going on?" Jonah suggested, because right now he just wanted to get rid of his sister.

"Jonah—what if I stop being invisible again? And they catch me?" Katherine asked. Suddenly she had tears in her eyes.

She's that upset? Jonah marveled. *That scared?*

Katherine was only a year younger than Jonah. She'd been a force of nature in his life for as long as he could remember, constantly flouncing in and out of the house, tagging along after him and his friends, tattling, "Jonah hurt my feelings! Make him let me play with him!" The minute Katherine walked into a room, Jonah always knew right away if she was happy or sad or angry or worried or frightened or ecstatic. And if Jonah or Mom or Dad didn't pick up on all the cues right away, she spelled it out for them, in diatribes that could last hours.

Was it possible that Katherine had changed too? In the midst of all their time traveling and getting lost and risking their lives and saving their friends' lives and never knowing if everything was going to work out—was it possible that Katherine had actually learned how to hide her emotions? Some of them, anyway?

A tear rolled down her cheek, and she wiped it away without saying a word.

She shivered, and didn't say anything about that, either.

"Here, uh, Katherine, I bet you're really cold," Jonah said. "You can wear my cloak."

He started to take it off, but even more tears welled in her eyes. Suddenly it seemed more important to make her laugh than to comfort her.

"Or—you could wrap this canvas blanket around yourself," Jonah said, lifting an edge of the canvas they'd been sitting on. "I bet it only *smells* like it's carried dead fish across the ocean." He wrapped the canvas around himself, to demonstrate. "See? It's almost like a Snuggie—"

He stopped, because there was something under the canvas. Something flat and smooth. . . . He pulled out a packet wrapped and tied in some sort of dried animal skins. He peeled back the skins to find papers inside.

"Maybe somebody has been leaving coded messages up here!" Katherine said excitedly.

"I don't think it's coded," Jonah whispered, staring

down at the papers. "I think it's flat-out true."

He'd already read the first sentence:

SoMetHing very strange and dangerouse ys happyning on The Discoverie. . . .

THIRTEEN

"Maybe JB figured out how to leave us written messages, even though he can't get through to us on the Elucidator," Katherine said hopefully. She started to reach for the papers, so she could see them too. Then her face fell. "Or—maybe it's Second again."

Second had left them written messages before, back in 1600. Second's messages had always been short—and manipulative.

This message was long and written in an old-fashioned script.

"I don't think Second would go to this much effort to make his message look like it belongs in 1611," Jonah said. "He always wanted us to know it was him, when he contacted us before. I think—I think someone actually on the ship right now wrote this."

He was scanning the rest of the words as quickly as he could:

Conditions have beene difficult and troubling from the time we left Lundon on the 17th of April, in the Year of Our Lord, 1610. The men have fought over coats, over bread, over which way a tossed hammer may land. . . . The master ys like a straw in the wind, favoring first one man, then another, deciding nothing, angering all. I believe he has secrets he chooses not to reveal. But those secrets may be the death of us all.

I have many reasons to fear for my lyfe, as I lie gravely ill, and there is little hope that I will see the shoares of my beloved homeland again. But I do not fear death. I am reconciled to my fate. What I cannot reconcile is the fear that the storie of this voyage will be told only by those who betray its purpose. Deception walks on the Discoverie; mutiny lurks in the minds and souls of cowards. I believe the evil plans will come to fruition soon. . . .

"Aw, it's just about the mutiny that already happened," Jonah said disappointedly, lowering the papers. "This doesn't help us at all."

"It could tell us what caused the mutiny," Katherine said. "The background. So maybe we can see where time went off track. What's that saying social studies teachers are always yammering on about—something like 'Those who don't remember history are forced to repeat it'?"

"That is *not* the reason we're stuck in 1611," Jonah said defensively.

But what if it was? What if JB should have paid more attention to what happened to Henry Hudson and his mutiny? Could that have made JB notice that Second was going to rebel against him?

"Here," Jonah said. "If you think these papers are so important, *you* read them." He thrust the papers into Katherine's hands and gazed around. "I'll watch out for icebergs."

What he really wanted to do was pull out the drawing of Andrea he'd tucked in his pocket and stare at it. But he couldn't do that in front of Katherine. He was sure he could feel the picture in his pocket, though, rustling a little, reminding him, *This isn't just about you and Katherine and JB and Second and time. Andrea's life depends on you fixing 1611 too.*

But how was he supposed to know how to fix anything? There weren't even any tracers anymore, to show how time was supposed to go.

"It's weird—this guy never gives his name, but he says he's going to hide notes all around the ship, so the true story of the *Discovery* will get out even if all the good people are killed," Katherine told him as she pored over the papers. "Why wouldn't he give his name, so people would know to believe him?"

"That's not so weird," Jonah argued. "Don't you think the mutineers would have killed him if they found the stuff he hid?"

"They tried to kill him *anyway*," Katherine said. "Don't you think? Don't you think he was probably one of the sick guys in the shallop with us?"

Jonah tried to think if any of them had looked particularly sneaky, as if they'd left behind secret notes.

They'd all just looked as though they were about to die.

"What's 'perfidy'?" Katherine asked, still studying the papers.

"How would I know?" Jonah asked irritably.

"It must be something bad," Katherine said. "This guy says the *Discovery* is full of it. Oh, here it is again, sort of— he calls his shipmates 'perfidious cretins'—no way that's a good thing."

How could Katherine think about vocabulary words

at a time like this? Jonah shifted uncomfortably on the creaky wood platform.

Just think about being a lookout. Watch out for danger. But how was he supposed to see danger coming when everything around them was a sea of gray?

"Boy!" someone shouted from down below. "See you land to the west?"

They had to be yelling at him.

"Um, uh . . . ," he called back. "I'm looking!"

First Jonah had to figure out which direction was west. He got a little help with that because Abacuk Prickett, who'd apparently been the one to yell, was standing down on the deck, pointing. Jonah squinted off into the distance. Were those dark, indistinct shapes land?

"Uh, yes!" he called back. "I mean, aye! I think so!" He squinted harder. "But it's, like, broken in the middle. Straight west—there's a gap!"

"A gap?" Prickett called back. "Think you that it's a passage? It must be!"

"Jonah, look," Katherine whispered, holding out the papers toward him.

"Shh. I'm trying to hear—," Jonah whispered back.

But down below, Prickett had already turned away. He was clapping Henry Hudson on the back, shaking Hudson's hand.

"Huh," Jonah muttered. "Looks like they're best buds

now. *I'm* the one who saw the gap. Er—passage."

"Jonah, *read* this," Katherine insisted, holding the paper right in front of his eyes, so he couldn't avoid it. She pointed to three sentences at the very bottom:

Of all the untrustworthy scoundrels on this ship, Abacuk Prickett ys the worst of all. Believe nothing he tells you; turn your back on him only if you wish to have a knyfe plunged into it. He ys to be feared above all others.

Jonah looked back toward the deck. Henry Hudson was still standing there, gazing toward the southwest. But Abacuk Prickett was nowhere in sight.

The ropes tied around the crow's nest tightened, suddenly pulled taut. Puzzled, Jonah leaned out, trying to see the full range of rigging below him.

And there was Abacuk Prickett, already halfway up the ropes.

The "worst" scoundrel on the entire ship hadn't disappeared. He was climbing right toward Jonah and Katherine.

FOURTEEN

"Jonah!" Katherine whispered, looking in the same direction. "There's not going to be room for all three of us in the crow's nest!"

"Can't you climb down before he gets here?" Jonah asked. "Without bumping into—"

He stopped, because this wasn't even worth asking. Most of the way up the rigging was basically just a narrow rope ladder.

Jonah looked down again. Prickett was getting closer and closer.

"Climb on my back," Jonah told Katherine. "Hurry."

Katherine grimaced, but quickly tucked the papers back under the canvas so both her hands were free. She put her arms around Jonah's neck and started to lift her knees.

"You mean, piggyback?" she asked. "Or—should I get up on your shoulders? More out of the way?"

Jonah pictured this in his mind: Katherine perched on his shoulders while he stood in the crow's nest, hundreds of feet off the ground, the ship swaying beneath them. If the ship hit a particularly rough wave, and Jonah or Katherine lost their balance for even a second, would Katherine topple over completely, out of the crow's nest, pulling Jonah down with her?

"Just on my back," Jonah muttered, through gritted teeth.

Katherine climbed on. Jonah locked his arms around her knees, and crossed his hands over his stomach—he hoped that didn't look too unnatural. He backed up, trying to take up as little of the room in the crow's nest as possible.

"Stay like that," Katherine whispered.

Jonah realized she was sitting precariously on the narrow railing. This worked—as long as she could hold on to him.

Prickett's weathered face appeared at the opposite edge of the crow's nest.

"Stand aside, boy," Prickett said irritably. "Make room for your betters."

Jonah leaned away from Prickett—which leaned

Katherine out even more, far over the edge of the crow's nest. She tightened her grip around Jonah's neck and let out a soft gasp.

"What's that, boy? Did you say something?" Prickett asked, climbing into the crow's nest. Unlike the technique Katherine and Jonah had used—landing mostly on their hands, and then turning over right side up, trying to dodge the mast—Prickett's movements were confident and effortless. He entered the crow's nest as easily as if he were merely striding into a room.

"N-no, sir," Jonah stammered. "Do you wish to see the land and the passage?"

He braced himself and Katherine against the railing, and lifted one arm to point. His cloak puffed up oddly, trapped against Katherine's arms encircling his neck. Jonah hastily pulled the cloak back into place.

Prickett didn't see that, Jonah told himself. *The mast blocked him. And he was already looking toward the land. Wasn't he?*

"The passage *does* exist," Prickett murmured. "Just as your father always believed."

Prickett spread his hands wide apart along the railing. He shifted his feet, taking up more of the crow's nest. Jonah would have felt crowded in the tiny space even if he hadn't had Katherine balanced on his back, leaning out over the rail.

"And there's no sight of land to the north or south or east?" Prickett asked, turning quickly.

Katherine was perched on the railing to the south. Prickett leaned impatiently around Jonah, in that direction.

"Stand *aside*, boy," he commanded.

His hand was about an inch from Katherine's knee.

Jonah grabbed Katherine's legs with both hands and slid her around to the right, toward the rigging. He let go with one hand and motioned behind his back, pointing down.

Katherine, this is not the time to be dense, he thought. *Or scared or slow. Get out of here! Climb down!*

He felt Katherine let go of his shoulders.

"Yes, yes, just as I expected," Prickett said, moving around as he peered first to the south, then to the north and east. "Nothing in sight except to the west. Well, I've seen enough. I shall climb down now. Pray allow me passage."

Jonah froze. He was pretty sure "pray allow me passage" actually meant "Get out of my way." But Katherine had just started climbing down. She was still tugging on Jonah's cloak even as Prickett said "allow." If Prickett went down now, he'd run right into her.

Maybe even knock her off the ropes.

"Uh, sir!" Jonah said, standing up straight. He pointed

in the opposite direction. "Look over there! Did you see—er, I mean, see you—the, uh . . ."

Way back at the beginning of this whole time-travel mess, before Jonah knew anything about what was going on, Jonah had fooled an FBI agent with the old "Look over there! What's that?" ploy. He'd made up an imaginary plane crash, a ball of flame—he'd been downright inspired. But what in the world was he supposed to claim he saw out here, where there was nothing but gray sky and gray sea and gray fog? Land? They'd already established that the only land was off to the west. Some sort of animal? Would they have whales out here? Polar bears? Would they have been called polar bears in 1611?

Jonah settled on a feeble "Is that a fish?"

"A *fish*?" Prickett repeated. "*One* fish? You would have me believe you can see one fish swimming in this water, from their height?"

"I mean, fishes. A school of fish," Jonah said quickly. He thought quickly. "Shouldn't we go fishing? For more food?"

Prickett glared suspiciously at him, then took him by the shoulders and moved him aside.

"Out of my way! I shall report you to the captain for insolence!" Prickett threatened. "Mocking an officer. For shame!"

"No, no, I wasn't mocking!" Jonah insisted, darting

back to block Prickett's way again. "I was . . . letting you know important information! Doing my job as lookout!"

Prickett's glare intensified. Then he slammed his hands against Jonah's chest, shoving him sideways.

"The captain shall be informed about *all* of this," he said.

And then he began climbing down the rigging.

Where was Katherine?

Prickett's bulk blocked her from view. Jonah knew she couldn't have gotten far, but was she climbing really, really fast? Could she get down to the deck before Prickett ran into her?

Prickett handled the ropes as if he'd been racing up and down rigging his whole life. Which he probably had. He even paused every few handholds to glance down— and still seemed to be setting some unbeatable record for speed.

Prickett turned to the side for an instant, perhaps to get one last glimpse of the land. In that moment Jonah saw something glow right below him—Katherine. Her hands were only one rung below Prickett's feet. Katherine glanced up, then glanced down quickly. Jonah could almost see her calculating: *I'm too high up to jump. I'd break a leg if I tried that.*

As Prickett stepped down to the next rung, Katherine

swung out of the way, holding on only to the sides of the rigging. Her feet dangled in midair.

Doesn't Prickett feel the ropes pulling over to the right? Jonah wondered.

He must have, because he stopped momentarily, his head turned directly toward Katherine. He even reached over to the side rope, Katherine just barely sliding her hands out of the way in time.

Ouch! Jonah thought. *That's got to cause some serious rope burn!*

Prickett seemed to be waiting for something.

Katherine twisted her face into a grimace. Jonah began to wonder how much upper-body strength she had.

Has she done weight training in gym class yet? He thought. *Not that that would really help, but . . .*

Jonah realized Katherine wasn't grimacing in pain. She was glaring at Prickett. And then—in a quick flash—she stuck her tongue out at him.

Prickett went back to climbing, out of Katherine's way. Katherine put her feet back on the ropes and waited for him to go on.

They still hadn't heard from JB, they still hadn't seen any tracers, and the "passage" they had seen seemed like even more proof that time was messed up beyond repair. Compared with all of that, it was no big deal that they'd managed to survive their encounter with Prickett.

Still, Jonah felt like cheering.

Prickett reached the deck. He strolled over to confer with Henry Hudson. And then Hudson leaned his head back and screamed up toward the crow's nest:

"John Hudson! Report to the deck! Immediately!"

Jonah lost the urge to cheer.

FIFTEEN

Jonah's legs almost buckled under him when he landed on the deck. It was partly exhaustion—climbing down the rigging hurt. But exhaustion alone didn't account for the way every muscle in his body threatened to give way.

Didn't ships' captains used to beat people with whips? he wondered, his knees trembling. *Beat them until they were almost dead, over nothing?*

Or was that just pirate *captains?*

He hoped it was just pirates.

Henry Hudson was glaring down at Jonah with his eyes narrowed, his mouth set into a thin, disapproving line.

He certainly looked like he wanted to beat someone.

"I can explain," Jonah said, which usually worked with his own parents back home.

At least it worked if Jonah didn't accidentally say something that got him into worse trouble.

Henry Hudson's eyes only grew angrier; his mouth flattened completely.

"Speak not," he said in a cold, hard voice. "I have heard all I wish."

He turned slightly toward Prickett, who was standing right beside him. Prickett gave a curt nod.

That's not fair! Jonah wanted to protest. *Whatever happened to accused criminals having the right to tell their side? Having the right to be considered innocent until proven guilty?*

Jonah realized nothing had happened to those rights. They just didn't exist yet in 1611.

It's not like I'm an accused criminal, anyhow, Jonah thought.

Hudson's glare made him feel like one.

Jonah tried to look at him adoringly, like a loving son. There was a trick to this, which Jonah sometimes used with his own parents. You blinked once or twice with a vacant, slightly goofy look on your face, and your parents forgot about whatever stupid thing you'd just done and started thinking instead about how cute you'd looked as a toddler, about how much they were going to miss you when you went off to college.

Evidently this trick didn't work with the John Hudson mask.

Or maybe Henry Hudson had never liked his son, not even when he was a cute little toddler. Maybe Henry Hudson wouldn't miss his son when he went off to . . . well, wherever you went after growing up as a ship's boy.

"I—," Jonah began.

Behind Hudson and Prickett, Jonah caught a glimpse of movement: It was Katherine, frantically shaking her head no.

Even Jonah could figure out what she meant: *Stop talking. Now. Or else.*

Hudson slapped his hand against the mast.

"I said, speak not!" he roared. "You have just earned yourself the harshest of punishments!"

He is going to beat me, Jonah thought, swaying slightly.

"When the others receive their noontime rations," Hudson said, pronouncing the judgment in a voice colder than the wind, "you shall receive nothing."

Huh? Jonah thought, trying to make sense of "noontime rations." *So that's . . . no food? I don't have to pretend to eat green, rotty meat? All right! Sounds like a reward, not a punishment! I'll just have Katherine sneak something better to me later. . . .*

He remembered that he needed to look like this punishment devastated him.

"I'm sorry!" he cried. "Please—"

Hudson struck him across the face.

"You do not mock your father's authority!" he screamed. "I am the captain!"

"Aye, aye," Jonah said, resisting the urge to put his hand against his stinging cheek. He cleared his throat. "Aye, aye, sir."

For a moment he worried that this wasn't the right thing to say to a ship's captain in 1611. Maybe "aye, aye, sir" came later. Maybe it would be seen as just more mockery.

But the look in Hudson's eye softened a bit.

"That's better," he said.

Jonah let out the breath he'd been holding without even realizing it.

Dear old "Dad" has just been thrown off his own ship and then let back on just because of some weird mess with time and history, Jonah reminded himself. *He's bound to be a little bit touchy about the whole authority thing.*

"Swab the deck!" Hudson commanded. "Now!"

"Yes, sir!" Jonah snapped back, trying once again for the very, very obedient military-recruit tone.

Someone placed a bucket and mop in his hands.

Jonah looked up and realized it was Staffe, the man who'd taken his side back in the shallop.

Staffe leaned close to Jonah's ear. From where Hudson and Prickett were standing, it probably looked as though

Staffe were just making sure that Jonah had a firm grip on the bucket handle.

But Staffe was whispering.

"Don't stand up for us," he said in a barely audible tone. "Don't try to help. It won't do any good. Not now."

And then Staffe turned and walked away, back to repairing a row of pegs on the rail.

Jonah almost dropped the bucket.

What was that all about? he wondered.

SIXTEEN

"Prickett's out to get you," Katherine said.

Jonah shoved the mop forward, then pulled it back.

"I could have figured that out all by myself," Jonah said. "And I'm not even invisible, and I can't go around listening to what people say without being seen."

The coils of dingy braided cloth that made up the mop head got caught on a rough place in the wood, and Jonah had to bend over and pull it free. Jonah could have sworn he could feel someone watching him, but when he straightened up, there was no one else there besides him and Katherine. The leaders of the ship—Hudson, Prickett, and King—had retreated into the captain's cabin to eat their lunch; the rest of the crew had disappeared into the hold. The weather had warmed up slightly, enough that the water he was swabbing on the deck didn't instantly turn to ice. But it still wasn't a great day for sitting out in the open air eating lunch.

Or for dipping your hands again and again into a cold bucket of water, Jonah thought sourly.

It wasn't fair that he was stuck mopping, while Katherine could just stand there watching.

Jonah made a mocking face at his sister, and rolled his eyes just for good measure.

"Okay, genius, if you're so brilliant, tell me this: *Why is Prickett out to get you?*" Katherine said. "That's what I can't figure out. I heard everything Prickett told Hudson about what you did in the crow's nest—which everybody's calling the *top*, for some reason. He made it sound like you practically spit in his eye and defied him and swore at him like . . . well, like a sailor."

"The liar!" Jonah said. He tightened his grip on the mop handle and hit the mop head against the deck with unnecessary force.

"It took you forever to get down here," Katherine said. "Prickett had time to tell John King he thought Nicholas Symmes should be promoted to first boy, ahead of you. And to tell that scary-looking cook person that you lost one of the fishing rods. You didn't even touch a fishing rod, did you?"

"*I* didn't," Jonah said. "But maybe the real John Hudson, before he vanished . . ."

Jonah shoved the mop harder. He was okay as long as he focused on minor actions: mopping, moving the bucket, snarling at Katherine. But if he let his thoughts creep toward anything approaching a broader viewpoint, he started feeling weak-kneed and panicked again.

Whatever the real John Hudson did before I got here, that's going to affect me, Jonah thought. *And so does whatever happened that made the ship come back for the shallop instead of letting us float off into nothingness . . . and whatever Second wanted to accomplish in 1611, when he changed 1600 . . . and whatever happened to JB that he can't even talk to us through the Elucidator anymore. . . . Aaah! I don't know what any of it means!*

The mop got caught on the rough wood again, and Jonah bent over it. The weird sensation of being watched hit him once more—he whirled around quickly, but it was only Katherine standing there, looking frighteningly see-through.

Jonah tried not to actually look at her, since he didn't like seeing her as glass.

"It's too weird, having you look and sound like someone else," Katherine mumbled.

Great. Each of them creeped out the other.

"I'm going to go listen at the captain's door, to see if I can hear anything Prickett and Hudson and King are saying," Katherine said. "And then I'm going to look around

the ship and see if there are any other notes hidden anywhere. Maybe the crow's nest letter writer left a note
somewhere about why Prickett hates John Hudson."

"Maybe," Jonah muttered. His stomach growled and
he added, "See if you can find a nice pepperoni pizza
lying around the ship while you're at it, okay?"

Katherine slugged his arm. At least *that* felt normal.

"I think I'll be doing well to find a few bread crumbs
that aren't covered with mold," she muttered as she left.
"*And* that they don't have counted, that they won't miss."

How could the Discovery *have gotten so low on food?* Jonah
wondered.

It was a stupid thought, just because back home he was
so used to having food available any time he wanted it.
He gazed out at the gray horizon—of course food would
be scarce here. It was too cold for much of anything to
grow on the land. Probably too cold for much of anything
to come from the sea. And if they'd left England in April
of 1610, that was fourteen months ago. How could they
have carried more than fourteen months worth of food?

And what would happen to him and Katherine if
everyone was just going to starve?

Jonah applied himself to diligently mopping the deck,
because that was a way to fight against all the worries.

"Psst," someone called behind him.

Jonah turned around. It was Staffe, carrying a tray toward the captain's cabin. He was looking around fearfully.

"I've been watching for the right moment . . . ," he whispered.

As he walked past, he slipped something into Jonah's hand.

"Cheese," Staffe murmured. "So you can eat, after all."

So Staffe's been watching me this whole time? Jonah wondered. He hoped he hadn't looked too suspicious, talking to Katherine. He eagerly closed his hand around the cheese, his mouth already watering.

But the "cheese" was hard as a rock. If Jonah actually bit into it, he'd probably chip a tooth.

Still, Jonah was pretty sure Staffe was risking a lot by giving it to him.

"No, thank you," Jonah said, slipping the cheese back to Staffe. "You eat it. I—I'll take my punishment like a man."

That sounded like something someone would say in 1611, didn't it?

Staffe stared at him. The man had startlingly blue eyes that stood out in his scarred, chapped, scruffy face.

"The wrong Hudson is leading this ship," Staffe whispered. Then he looked around nervously, as if fearing someone else might have heard. But even Katherine was out of earshot—she was way across the deck now, her ear pressed against the door of Hudson's cabin.

Wrong Hudson leading . . . , Jonah thought. *Was that what was going on between John Hudson and his dad? Did lots of people think* John *should have led a mutiny? Is that how the mutiny went wrong? No—not if John Hudson was supposed to end up in the shallop.*

Jonah's head was starting to hurt from trying to figure everything out. Staffe turned to walk away.

"No—wait," Jonah said desperately. "I have to ask you—"

But what could he ask that the real John Hudson wouldn't have already known? *Why does Prickett hate me?* Nope. *Why are you and I such great buddies?* Nope. *What else am I supposed to do as ship's boy besides going up in the crow's nest and swabbing the deck?* Nope.

And then he knew what he could ask.

He dug in his pocket and pulled out the drawing of Andrea. He resisted the temptation to stand there gazing at it for a few minutes before showing it to Staffe.

"Look," he said. "I found this. See—it says this girl joined a tribe. What tribe do you think she joined?"

Jonah thought he'd worked up a pretty clever plan in just a few seconds. Whatever Staffe answered, Jonah could say, "Will you write that down?" And then Jonah could look at his handwriting and see if it was the same as on the papers in the crow's nest. At least that was one mystery Jonah might be able to solve.

But Staffe snatched the paper away, hiding it from view.

"You ripped this from one of your father's books?" Staffe asked, his words weighted with as much horror as if he'd just discovered that Jonah had killed someone.

"No!" Jonah protested automatically. "Well, actually . . . yeah, I kind of did. But not on purpose! It was an accident!"

This was true. In his very first moments after arriving in 1611 he'd brushed away something he felt against his face, heard paper rip, and realized that he'd torn out this page from a book. It'd been his first clue that Andrea and his other friends had survived 1600—and that their actions had changed time.

The picture never would have existed in original time.

"Your father worships his books!" Staffe muttered. He looked around frantically, as if searching for a place to hide the evidence of what Jonah had done.

Jonah's brain was running a little behind. He and Katherine had been so vague and out of it in their first few moments on the ship—and then they'd rushed so quickly into dealing with the mutiny. What had happened to the rest of that book?

And what would Henry Hudson do if he found out that Jonah had torn out this page?

Staffe was acting as though this changed everything—as though Jonah's very life might be in danger.

Jonah reached out for the paper, because he didn't like the way Staffe was crumpling it.

"Well, don't tell anyone what happened, okay?" Jonah said, even though he was pretty sure people didn't say "okay" in 1611. "It's just, this girl . . ."

A bit of sympathy crept into Staffe's expression.

"The girl," he said, almost gently. "Of course. We all miss seeing females, and for a young lad like yourself . . ."

Jonah's fingers brushed the paper, but Staffe pulled it away, out of reach.

"If I give this back to you, you'll get caught with it," Staffe said. "You'll forget; you'll pull it out just to look when others are around. . . ."

"No, I won't," Jonah said.

Staffe shook his head. And even though Staffe had sunken cheeks and numerous scars and a long, ratty beard that whipped around in the wind—and so looked absolutely nothing like Jonah's clean-shaven, unscarred, slightly overweight father—for a moment Jonah had a flash of feeling like he was back home, waiting for his dad to tell him, once again, "Jonah, you're a kid. You're a good kid, and there are a lot of decisions your mother and I trust you to make on your own. But—this isn't one of them."

Staffe took three steps, over to the railing. And then, before Jonah could stop him, he dropped Andrea's picture into the water.

SEVENTEEN

"What'd you do that for?" Jonah demanded, rushing toward the railing.

"For your own good," Staffe said, sounding just like Jonah's dad again.

It always made Jonah furious when his dad said it, too.

"That was valuable!" Jonah said. "Priceless!"

He wasn't even thinking about what the paper represented, the way the paper was evidence of how Second had changed time. The way that, if Jonah held on to it and kept looking at it, maybe it could become evidence that Jonah and Katherine had fixed time.

All Jonah could think was, *What if I never see Andrea again? And now I don't even have her picture anymore. . . .*

He leaned far out over the railing.

"I'll jump in and get it," he said.

But the waves had already washed over the paper, dragging it out of sight. And, well, Jonah had seen *Titanic*. He knew: People died in a matter of minutes in water that cold.

The door of Hudson's cabin opened suddenly, making both Staffe and Jonah jump. Jonah almost *fell* over the railing.

"Were you bringing the captain's tray?" Prickett asked Staffe. "Or merely laying about, chatting with the miscreant?"

"Miscreant" was yet another word Jonah had never heard before, but he could just tell by the way Prickett said it that he was supposed to be insulted.

"Bringing the tray," Staffe said. "Sir."

He rushed toward Prickett. Prickett took the tray from him and said, "Begone from my sight."

Jonah expected Prickett to shut the door again, giving Jonah and Staffe more chance to talk. But Prickett kept standing there watching.

"It would be wise for you to be careful about whom you associate with," Prickett told Staffe.

"Yes, sir," Staffe said, backing away.

Staffe reached the stairway and went scurrying down into the hold. And still Prickett kept standing in the doorway.

Jonah saw Katherine slip past him, into Hudson's cabin.

She was shaking her head and frowning at Jonah—she must have seen everything that had happened between him and Staffe.

And *then* Prickett stepped aside and let the door slide shut behind him.

Jonah went back to swabbing the deck, but this time the action didn't soothe him at all.

Andrea's picture is gone, he thought, angrily shoving the mop around. *And Katherine is alone in that cabin with crazy Henry Hudson and awful Abacuk Prickett and even John King, who seemed so eager to pull out his sword and start slicing it through the air back during the mutiny. . . .*

Jonah kept pushing the mop back and forth, but his eyes were playing tricks on him in the pools of water on the wet wood. He could see each and every time that invisibility had failed to protect them—or even put them in greater danger—during their previous trips through history.

At the Tower of London guards had thrust flaming torches at them—even setting a small lock of Katherine's hair on fire before Jonah managed to put it out.

At the Battle of Bosworth, Katherine had suddenly fallen down, and Jonah had been certain she'd been hit by a flying arrow.

And at Westminster Abbey, Jonah and Katherine and their

friends Chip and Alex had suddenly lost their invisibility—right in front of the king of England.

Katherine's invisibility was even less reliable here and now, when everything about time travel was messed up. What would happen if she suddenly became visible in Captain Hudson's cabin? If he and the others caught her spying?

Jonah broke out in a cold sweat.

He shoved his mop closer to Captain Hudson's door. If someone came out, it would just look as though he was cleaning this side of the deck, right? He looked around quickly and, seeing no one coming from belowdecks, he pressed his ear against the door.

All he could hear was a low rumble of voices.

". . . the passage . . ."

". . . loaded with treasure . . ."

". . . sailors we trust . . ."

It was frustrating, to catch only about three words of every ten. He couldn't blame Katherine for wanting to dart inside.

". . . divide up . . ."

Were they planning to divide the treasures, or divide the sailors?

"Oh, no!" Prickett cried suddenly in a startled voice. "What's that?"

They'd found Katherine. That was the only explanation.

Jonah rammed his shoulder against the door, forcing it open. It gave way more easily than he expected.

Jonah landed flat on the floor of Henry Hudson's cabin.

EIGHTEEN

Jonah looked up to see everyone circled around him: Hudson, Prickett, King—and the still-invisible Katherine.

Katherine was shaking her head in despair and mouthing the words, *What were you thinking?*

The others just looked furious.

"Caught listening at doors," Prickett muttered darkly. "Eavesdropping."

"No," Jonah said, thinking hard. "I wasn't. I—"

He decided to buy some time—and a little dignity— by trying to stand up. But Prickett quickly grabbed Jonah's mop and pressed the handle against Jonah's chest, pinning him to the ground.

"He lies," Prickett accused.

"No, really," Jonah said, wishing he *could* come up with a good lie. The mop dripping against his chest gave him an idea. "I was just leaning against the door, trying to get the best angle to—er—swab the corners of the deck. I wasn't eavesdropping at all! Didn't hear a thing!"

It was so frustrating telling a lie with John Hudson's voice. It came out sounding squeaky and untrustworthy.

Not that Jonah's real voice would have worked any better.

"We must make an example of him," Prickett said.

The year 1611 wasn't one of those times when people had their hands cut off for stealing, was it? If so, the punishment for eavesdropping might be . . . what? Having an ear cut off?

Jonah lifted his hands to grab both his ears, which probably made him look even guiltier.

"Please," Jonah said. "F-father . . ."

He was appealing to Hudson, but Hudson's eyes wheeled about, his gaze lighting first on Prickett, then King.

He wouldn't look directly at Jonah.

"We could bring out the stocks," Prickett said. "Put him right in the middle of the deck, for all to see."

Stocks? Jonah thought frantically. He looked at Katherine, hoping she would know what this meant. If it was too bad, maybe he needed to jump up and try to escape.

Though, where could he escape *to?*

Katherine looked every bit as baffled as Jonah felt. She was mouthing something else now—maybe, *I'll rescue you if I have to?*

It was virtually impossible to lip-read her almost-invisible lips.

John King reached down and grabbed Jonah by the shoulders, holding him so tightly that Jonah wouldn't have been able to escape, regardless. King hustled Jonah out of the cabin.

"All hands on deck!" Hudson called down into the hold. "Immediately!"

"Bring the ill and the lame, too!" Prickett called behind him.

Including all the sickest people meant that "immediately" took a long time. Jonah stood shivering in John King's grasp.

"Really, I didn't—," Jonah tried again.

"Silence!" King growled, and struck him across the face so hard that it jarred Jonah's teeth.

He decided silence might be a good idea, though he kept looking around, trying to figure out what punishment Prickett and Hudson and King intended to give him.

Mutineers always hang, Hudson had said, just that morning. But surely being caught eavesdropping wasn't considered mutiny, was it?

Finally the rest of the crew was assembled on the deck. In the past hour or so Jonah had stopped feeling so horrified at the sight of scars and missing teeth and oozing sores. But the whole crew, all together, was hideous. They were walking skeletons covered in rags. They were skin diseases stretched over bone. They were death masks come to life.

In the twenty-first century, every single one of them would be in a hospital bed, Jonah thought. *In an isolation unit, probably.*

Beside him Katherine took a step back.

"Hear ye, hear ye!" Hudson cried. "This boy shows no respect for the ship's rules! Therefore, he is sentenced to the stocks until sundown tomorrow!"

"Sun don't go down until practically the middle of the night around here, this time of year," Staffe muttered.

"I am well aware of that fact," Hudson said, a dangerous edge to his voice. "Since you seem to doubt my knowledge as much as this boy doubts my authority, would you care to join him in the stocks?"

Staffe looked straight into Jonah's eyes. Then he looked away.

"No," he said.

Jonah heard a rolling sound behind him, some sort of contraption being moved forward. John King shoved down on his shoulders, forcing Jonah onto his knees. And then King yanked Jonah's head forward.

Jonah's throat hit hard wood.

If "stocks" is just an old-fashioned word for "guillotine," Katherine would figure out how to stop this before anyone actually kills me. Wouldn't she? Jonah wondered dizzily.

Someone pulled Jonah's hands forward, his wrists slamming against wood now too.

Jonah struggled to turn his head to look for Katherine—and to see what was going to happen to him next. He caught a quick glimpse of something descending toward his neck and wrists.

"Noooo!" he screamed.

NINETEEN

Jonah heard wood crashing against wood on either side of his head, but nothing hit him.

The hands that had been holding him let go. For a long moment Jonah stayed with his shoulders hunched forward, braced for pain.

None came. Nothing else happened.

Jonah dared to lift his head, ever so slightly. The back of his head bumped against wood. But it was just a bump—nothing painful.

Jonah cautiously turned his head side to side. His neck and wrists were trapped in a wooden frame. What he'd seen falling was the top part of the frame being lowered against the bottom part.

And now he could see John King fastening a lock at the end of that frame, holding everything together, keeping Jonah in place.

Oh, yeah, Jonah thought. *Now I know what stocks are. I've even been in them before!*

Several years ago—back in Jonah's real life, in the twenty-first century—Jonah's family had taken a vacation to Colonial Williamsburg. Jonah had clowned around in the wooden stocks while the guide droned on and on about old-timey forms of punishment. Jonah just hadn't bothered remembering what they were called.

So nothing about stocks actually hurt people, if they let tourists in them, Jonah reasoned. *So what's the point?*

"Behold this boy's shame," Hudson intoned solemnly. "Gaze ye up on his shame, and vow to follow a better path."

Shame? Jonah thought. *That's the point? That's all you've got?*

And yet . . . it *was* humiliating, to have the whole crew staring at him. He caught Staffe's eye, and the man's gaze was full of disappointment. Just a few minutes ago Staffe had thought well enough of Jonah to imply that he should be leading the ship. Now Staffe was looking at him as if he were a criminal.

I can explain, Jonah wanted to tell him. *It's not what you think!*

Only, Jonah couldn't explain. Not without bringing up time travel and his invisible sister, or admitting that he was only impersonating the real John Hudson. And those explanations would just make Staffe think he was crazy.

Staffe turned his back on Jonah.

Then the man who'd had a compass in the shallop—Wydowse?—turned his back as well.

Then other crew members did the same: one decrepit, ragged, skeletal man after the other refusing to look in Jonah's direction.

Jonah began shaking.

It's like they're saying I don't even exist for them, he thought. *Like I'm not worthy for them to see.*

Jonah turned his head, because he didn't want to watch all those people rejecting him. But he'd forgotten, and turned toward Hudson and Prickett and King.

Those were the last people he wanted to look at right now.

He had some pride. He kept his head up and his gaze defiant and didn't immediately whip his head back in the other direction. He wasn't going to give the three men any more reason to gloat over Jonah's shame.

Then Jonah realized none of the three men looked like they were gloating.

They looked . . . upset.

Hudson started to open his mouth, as if he was going to yell at the entire crew. But Prickett laid a warning hand on Hudson's arm.

"Don't," he said softly. Probably Hudson and Jonah were the only ones close enough to hear him. "Let it go. Sometimes silence is the greatest sign of power. Keep them guessing about when punishment may come for them."

What did *that* mean?

Jonah looked back and forth between the crew and the ship's leaders, and everything he'd thought before flipped upside down.

The men weren't turning their backs on Jonah because they were rejecting *him*.

They were rejecting his punishment.

Hudson had commanded them to look at Jonah's shame. And they were turning away so they didn't have to.

This is like—what's that thing teachers are always talking about at school? Where you rebel, but you don't do it by fighting? You use peaceful protest? Jonah couldn't remember the term. But it was what Gandhi had done, what Martin Luther King had done, what Nelson Mandela had done—or would, when the twentieth century showed up. If the twentieth century still existed.

Whoa, Jonah thought. *It's like I'm the leader of a movement!*

But didn't leaders of movements know what they were leading people toward?

TWENTY

"Back to work!" Hudson commanded, and *Discovery*'s crew scattered, leaving Jonah behind in the stocks.

As soon as everyone was out of easy earshot, Katherine knelt beside Jonah.

"Are you all right?" she wailed. "I'll get you out of there!"

She reached for the lock.

"Katherine, *no*," Jonah said. "Don't you know how that would look?"

He could imagine how the crew would view it: the key to the lock seeming to float out of John King's pocket, the top part of the stocks seeming to rise on its own, Jonah standing up and going free. It would look like magic.

Or witchcraft and bedevilment, as the one sailor had guessed way back at the beginning of the mutiny.

"But doesn't that hurt?" Katherine asked.

"Nah, I'm fine," Jonah said, trying to sound cheerful. "I can last until sunset tomorrow, no problem."

The truth was, he already had a crick in his neck from leaning forward, and his knees were starting to ache on the hard wood of the deck. And how cold would it get at night?

He plastered a smile on his face anyhow, for Katherine's benefit.

She frowned back at him.

"Why did you do that?" she asked.

"I thought you were in danger," Jonah mumbled. "I thought maybe you'd turned visible again. What *was* Prickett yelling about? When he said, 'Oh, no! What's that?'?"

Katherine's frown deepened, but now she seemed more upset at Hudson and Prickett than Jonah.

"They were looking at maps," Katherine said. "I don't know if this is a sign that time's really messed up or not, but they have some very strange ideas about what North and South America look like. I wouldn't have even been able to tell what those maps were, except that the shape of Florida was usually right."

"We're a long way away from Florida," Jonah muttered.

"Yeah—I think the other parts of those maps are just guesses," Katherine said. "What the explorers want to find." She looked thoughtful. "Every single one of those maps had this beautiful river connecting the Atlantic and Pacific oceans."

"You mean, like the Panama Canal?" Jonah asked.

"Not where Panama is," Katherine corrected him. "Right here." She pointed out toward the chilly water beyond the deck. Then she seemed to realize how ridiculous it was to match up a real place with mostly imaginary maps. "Or, at least, sort of in this area. Where Canada's going to be someday."

"That's the Northwest Passage, then," Jonah whispered. "What my 'father' wants to call the Hudson Passage." He shrugged, or tried to. It was kind of hard with his neck trapped in the stocks. "Well, they'll find out it doesn't exist. Um. Does it?"

"I don't think so," Katherine said, and it was odd for her to sound so uncertain. "Unless the ice caps melt, or something like that."

Jonah tried once again to remember what Mrs. Rorshas had said about the Northwest Passage back in fifth grade. Social studies had always been right after lunch, when the classroom seemed way too warm, and Jonah got sleepy. But there'd been a map on the wall that

Jonah had stared at sometimes to try to stay awake—had it shown a Northwest or Hudson Passage? Or did it just show the United States, not all of North America? Jonah could remember little stickers on the map for the Pony Express, the transcontinental railroad, the Oregon Trail, the battles of the American Revolution, the battles of the Civil War . . .

Wait a minute, Jonah thought. *Were the American Revolution and Civil War battles really on the same map?*

Or had Mrs. Rorshas switched out the maps as the year went along, depending on which time period they were studying?

Jonah hit one of his hands against the framework of the stocks.

"You said Prickett was upset about one of those maps?" he asked Katherine. "And he was acting surprised, like this was the first time he'd seen it?"

"Yeah," Katherine said. "He shouted—you heard him."

Jonah raised an eyebrow. At least he could do that much, even though he was in the stocks.

"The *Discovery* left England more than a year ago," he said. "They were stranded out here in the middle of nowhere all winter and spring. So . . ." Jonah paused for dramatic effect. "Where'd they get a new map?"

TWENTY-ONE

"Good question," Katherine said. This was perhaps the first time in Jonah's life that Katherine had acknowledged that he might have a working brain. She squinted over toward the other side of the deck, where Prickett and Hudson were standing near the rail.

Then her face smoothed out.

"Oh, duh," Katherine said. "They must have gotten the map from natives. Canadian Indians. Or whatever they're called. Inuits?"

Jonah wasn't ready to give up on showing off his brainpower. Especially if Katherine was going to unleash fancy words like *Inuits*.

"But what language was the map written in?" he asked.

Katherine went back to looking perplexed.

"English," she said. "Or, you know, that funny-looking

old-timey English, where everything's spelled weird, but you can mostly figure out what it means."

"How would natives out here have a map written in English?" Jonah asked, even though Katherine was clearly already trying to figure that out. "If anyone English had been here before, I think things would be different." He was enjoying himself now, and went for the heavy sarcasm. "Wouldn't the crew of the *Discovery* have gone to the English embassy for help over the winter, instead of almost starving and getting scurvy and everything?"

Katherine rolled her eyes, as if trying to make sure Jonah knew how stupid she thought his humor was.

"Maybe the map was passed from tribe to tribe, across the continent, starting from someone near Roanoke colony or Jamestown—is Jamestown there yet?" Katherine asked.

Jonah didn't have the slightest clue when the English founded Jamestown, so he settled for looking skeptical.

"We're, like, a billion miles away from Jamestown and Roanoke," he said sarcastically.

"Okay, then, some aliens came down from outer space and gave that map to Henry Hudson," Katherine said, plunging into sarcasm of her own. "Or gave it to some native, who gave it to Hudson. It was right before the aliens built the pyramids and developed the Mayan calendar."

Jonah jolted back, banging his head and wrists against the wood frame.

"It wasn't aliens," he said, totally serious now. "It was—"

"Time travelers," Katherine said, speaking with him, reaching the same conclusion at the same time. "Or a time trave*ler*," she added.

She always had liked getting in the last word. But Jonah wasn't going to worry about that now.

"Second would do that," Jonah said, all joking forgotten. "He changed 1600 for Virginia Dare and her grandfather. He wouldn't think twice about giving Henry Hudson a map he wasn't supposed to have. That map is one of the ways he's changing time."

"Yeah, but why?" Katherine asked, her eyes troubled. "What is he trying to make happen?"

Jonah peered back across the deck, toward Hudson. Jonah could see just the tip of some paper poking out of Hudson's fur coat—possibly even the map Katherine had been talking about.

Jonah was about 100 percent certain that it was because of Second that Hudson was there on the ship, back in control, continuing to explore, continuing to sail west—rather than drifting off into oblivion in the shallop, lost to history forever.

And it was because of Second that the mutineers who'd tried to overthrow Hudson were *not* standing on this deck, hightailing it back to England. Instead they were stranded on an ice floe somewhere—or already drowned.

Jonah grimaced. He didn't want to think about that. He went back to the broader perspective.

What does it matter which person or group is on the ship, in control, and which one is stranded in the ice? Jonah wondered. *What does it matter? Who cares?*

He realized that he'd heard kids asking those same questions in social studies class practically since kindergarten.

Er, did we have social studies in kindergarten? he asked himself. *First or second grade, anyway.*

Every year, sometimes even before the first week of school was over, somebody would complain, "This is boring! Why do we have to learn about old, dead people, anyhow?"

And that was always the cue for some long, boring lecture from the teacher, who, in the first week of school, still had starry-eyed dreams about Imparting Important Lessons and Opening Minds and Making Kids Care. (By the end of the year the teachers would mostly just grunt, "Because it's going to be on the test. That's why.")

Jonah had never actually paid attention to any of those boring lectures. Now he wished he had.

What if the teachers actually told us exactly how the world would be different if Henry Hudson found the Northwest Passage? Jonah wondered.

Over by the railing the sailors around Hudson and Prickett were pulling a rope out of the water.

"I told ye it would be deep enough!" Hudson said, with such excitement that his voice carried across the whole deck.

Jonah realized that they were entering the passageway he'd seen from the crow's nest. Flat, featureless land lay on two sides of the ship.

"Didn't you say that that river you discovered when you were sailing the *Half Moon* seemed deep enough at the beginning too?" Wydowse asked him.

"This is different," Hudson said. He put his hand over his heart, as if preparing to swear an oath.

Or maybe he was just holding on to the map in his pocket.

"This time it's certain," Prickett agreed. "I believe a toast is in order?"

He and Hudson and King and a few others went back toward Hudson's cabin.

None of them even glanced at Jonah as they walked by.

"I should follow them," Katherine said. "I have to hear what they're saying."

"Ye-es," Jonah agreed unhappily.

But what if something happened to her while he was trapped in the stocks and couldn't do a thing to help?

TWENTY-TWO

Jonah watched the door of Hudson's cabin. He watched the sailors creeping around the deck. He watched the flat land slide by.

Nothing happened.

Maybe shame isn't the worst part of being punished in the stocks, he thought. *Maybe you're just supposed to get so bored that you start saying, "Please! I'll do anything you want! Just let me out of here!"*

But maybe the stocks wouldn't have seemed so boring to the real John Hudson. Maybe he was used to boredom. Adults in the twenty-first century were always complaining about how Jonah's generation expected to be entertained all the time, constantly watching TV or hanging out online or listening to iPods.

An iPod would really help right now, Jonah thought irritably.

All I've got is an Elucidator that hasn't worked since . . . since . . .

When was the last time the Elucidator had worked? *Had* that really been JB's ghostly voice saying *Good job* in the shallop, or had Jonah just imagined it?

Somehow it seemed to matter. What if the last moment that the Elucidator worked was also the last moment that they'd had a chance to get time back on track?

Don't think like that, Jonah told himself.

"JB," he whispered urgently. "Please! Start talking to me again! Tell me what we're supposed to do!"

No answer. Thinking about the Elucidator had just made Jonah realize that a corner of it was poking into his chest. He tried to shift positions a little, but it was impossible to get comfortable with his neck and wrists trapped in the stocks.

"JB, please!" he whispered again. "If you can get us out of here, now would be a great time for it! Please!"

Too late Jonah realized that Staffe had come to stand nearby. How was Jonah supposed to explain what he'd just said?

"Oh, uh—," Jonah began.

Staffe cast an anxious glance toward the door of Hudson's cabin.

"It is good that you be praying," Staffe said.

"Er—yes," Jonah said, relieved that Staffe had misunderstood. Of course he would think of praying before he thought of talking to futuristic time-travel devices.

"God does forgive those who truly repent," Staffe said.

"I haven't done anything to repent *for*," Jonah protested. "I'm being punished unfairly! Falsely accused!"

Staffe regarded him levelly.

"You stole that page from your father's book," he said.

"No, I didn't!" Jonah insisted. "I just . . .Well, I can't explain, but—trust me on this one!"

Staffe kept looking directly into Jonah's eyes.

"I am trying to trust you," he finally said. "But as you know, this ship is a hard place to see what is right and what is wrong."

The door of Hudson's cabin cracked open, and Staffe nervously walked on. A burst of raucous laughter came from the cabin, as the door opened wider. A few more sailors stepped inside, and the door closed again.

Jonah was relieved to see that Katherine had stepped out of the cabin while the door was open. She stomped toward him, shaking her head.

"Remember how I always complained about walking past the boys' locker room at school, because you guys all stink so bad?" she said. "That's *nothing* compared with sitting in a tiny room with a bunch of sailors who probably haven't taken a bath in fourteen months. *And* they're all drinking something called aquavit, that makes them belch a lot. Ew, ew, ew!"

She pretended to gag.

"But did you find out anything?" Jonah asked.

"Yeah—Henry Hudson's got the biggest ego on the planet," Katherine said. "'My name shall be written on the tablets of the sea. . . . My name shall be written on the tablets of the sea'—he must have said that, like, fifty times. And Abacuk Prickett just kept encouraging him: 'Yes, master, you shall be the most famous sea captain of all time.' Made me want to turn visible just so I could say, 'Guess what? Four hundred years from now, schoolkids are just going to get you mixed up with Vasco da Gama on tests. The really stupid ones aren't going to remember your name even when the question is, 'Who discovered the Hudson River and the Hudson Bay?'"

Jonah thought maybe he'd done that once.

"But what if that isn't the question on tests four hundred years from now?" Jonah asked. "What if Second messing up time makes it so the question is always, 'Which discoverer found the Hudson Passage and changed history forever?' What if Henry Hudson becomes the explorer that every-one remembers, the way Christopher Columbus is now?"

Katherine stopped her rant.

"I don't know," she said. "I—I'm going to go look for

more secret messages and see if we can do anything."

Before Jonah had a chance to answer, she rushed down the stairs into the hold below.

Maybe Jonah wouldn't have noticed if he had been able to walk around too. But he could see what Katherine was doing: She was trying to keep moving, trying to keep busy, so she didn't have time to think about what a mess they were in.

Jonah had nothing but time to think.

I am trying to trust you, Staffe had said.

My name shall be written on the tablets of the sea, Hudson had said.

We didn't know what we were doing, JB had said. And then, later on, *We made even more mistakes than I thought.*

"But you still thought Katherine and I could fix everything, didn't you?" Jonah muttered. "Don't you still think that?"

It did no good to talk to JB, when Jonah knew he wasn't going to answer. Jonah would be better off actually praying, the way Staffe thought he was.

Just then some of the sailors over by the railing let out a shout. One of them scurried toward Hudson's cabin.

"Sir! Sir! We've spotted a savage in one of their odd little vessels—a kayak? What should we do?"

TWENTY-THREE

The native came onto the ship.

Jonah thought this was incredibly brave of him—there was only one of him, and more than twenty Englishmen. And surely the native had never seen anything as immense as the ship before.

But the man climbed calmly onto the deck and watched expressionlessly as Hudson advanced toward him.

"I am Henry Hudson, the great sea captain," Hudson said, tapping his chest.

"Ikau," the man said, pointing to his own chest, which was covered in a loose-fitting shirt of some sort of light-weight animal skin—seal, perhaps? He also wore matching pants and moccasins.

"Mayhap he'll have food to trade with us!" one of the sailors near Jonah whispered, a little too loudly. "Fresh-caught fowl or deer or . . ."

Hudson silenced the whispering sailor with just a glance.

"Know you where this river leads?" Hudson asked. "Does it go all the way to the great sea to the west?"

Ikau said nothing.

"The *river*," Hudson said, pointing out toward the water, and then moving his hands in a swimming motion, imitating the current.

"Yes, tell me about the river," Ikau said.

Jonah jerked back, hitting his head against the stocks yet again. He'd understood Ikau! How? How could Ikau possibly be speaking English?

Jonah realized that Hudson and all the other sailors were looking blankly at Ikau. They hadn't understood a word he'd said.

"Oo-oo-uh-nu-oo," one of the sailors muttered, imitating the sounds Ikau had made.

Ooooh, Jonah realized. *He's not speaking English. He's speaking whatever language he normally speaks. I just understand because JB gave Katherine and me those translation vaccines. It's like the way I could understand Algonquin back in 1600. And medieval English back in 1485.*

Should he volunteer to translate? How in the world would he possibly explain knowing Ikau's language?

"We are from England," Hudson said, speaking distinctly.

Whoa, Jonah thought. *Even in 1611 people think that if they just speak loud enough and slow enough, foreigners will understand them.*

Except, here, the English speakers were the foreigners.

"We are a strong and powerful people, and if you don't tell us what we want to know, we could kill you, just like that," Hudson said, snapping his finger.

Ikau blinked at the sudden sound. But when John King pointed a gun at him, he only looked at it with a mildly curious air, the same way he was regarding everything else on the ship.

So he's never seen a gun before? Jonah thought. *Should I translate, after all, just so he knows he's got to be careful?*

In a sudden, fluid movement Ikau pulled out a harpoon that he'd been hiding somewhere in his clothes. He pointed it straight at Henry Hudson and looked defiantly at everyone else around him.

Okay, he gets it, Jonah thought. *No translation needed.*

"You will tell me about the river!" Ikau thundered insistently.

Now, that was weird. Ikau lived here, didn't he? Wouldn't he already know about the river? Wouldn't he want the Englishmen to tell him about England, or their ship, or the gun, or stuff like that?

Ikau pulled his harpoon back a bit, as if he thought

the Englishmen might be too frightened of him to reply. Jonah realized suddenly why Ikau wasn't worried that there was just one of him and more than twenty Englishmen.

He sees how sickly everyone is. He probably thinks he could fight the entire crew and win, Jonah thought. *And maybe he could, if there wasn't a gun involved.*

"This river was not here!" Ikau said. "It was not here in my father's time or my father's father's time or my father's father's father's time. It was not here the last time I came this way! Who brought it? You? You, with your floating mountain of wood? Or did you just find it this way, like me? Who can carry away rocks and dirt and ice and trees and leave only a crater behind, for the water to fill?"

"What?" Jonah exploded. "What do you mean, the river wasn't here before?"

Everyone looked at him.

Uh-oh, Jonah thought. *Did I somehow manage to speak in Ikau's language by mistake?*

The astonished faces around him made him think that he had. He hadn't known the translator vaccines could work on speaking, as well as hearing. But he'd never actually had reason to try it out before.

Ikau looked as surprised as everyone else. He swung

his harpoon at the sailors near him and stepped closer to Jonah.

"You don't know about the river?" Ikau asked, a furrow appearing between his heavy brows. His deep-set eyes took in the wooden frame of the stocks, holding Jonah in place. "And you speak my language—and they have you trapped?"

"Pretty much," Jonah said. "It's kind of a long story."

Ikau looked around—from Jonah in the stocks to Hudson's self-important stance to the skeletal sailors to John King, with the gun pointing directly at him.

And then in a flash Ikau ran to the railing and scrambled over. A second later Jonah heard the muffled splash of an oar speeding through water.

"Shoot him!" Hudson commanded. "He's getting away! He might have stolen something! He might come back with a war party!"

King shot off the gun, but then he shook his head and tried again. And again. And again. Finally Hudson put his hand on King's arm.

"Hold your fire," Hudson said. "He's too far away now."

Jonah let out a silent sigh of relief.

But then Hudson turned toward Jonah.

"It appears my son has been hiding his talents from me," Hudson said. "I did not know he knew how to speak savage."

"I've just been . . . studying a little . . . on the side," Jonah mumbled.

"Then pray tell," Hudson commanded, glaring down at him. "Whatever did the savage reveal?"

TWENTY-FOUR

Jonah looked for Katherine in the crowd. Surely she'd heard the commotion on the deck; surely she'd raced up the stairs to see what was going on—surely she'd have a better idea than he did about what he should say.

But when he caught a glimpse of Katherine's see-through face behind a bunch of sailors, she looked just as worried and confused as Jonah felt.

"Um," Jonah began. He gnawed on his lip and tried to figure out what to say next.

"I, too, know a bit of the savage tongue," Prickett said, stepping between Jonah and the captain. "The boy was only speaking doggerel." Prickett laughed, lightly, in a way that made Jonah seem ridiculous. "But I believe the savage was saying that the river is wide for many leagues ahead, until it spills into a vast sea none of his people have traveled. Isn't that correct, boy?"

Prickett turned to look at Jonah. Jonah opened his mouth. But Prickett was already turning his back on him again.

"But what am I saying?" Prickett murmured, with a shrug. "The boy will only lie. Why should I ask him?"

Jonah's face burned.

"Come," Prickett said, taking Hudson's arm. "Is not this cause for more celebration?"

But Hudson pulled his arm from Prickett's grasp.

"I should like to see the scope of this passageway with mine own eyes," Hudson said. "I shall stand lookout in the top."

"Sir, your bad knee—," Prickett began.

"It is not that bad," Hudson said.

"As you wish, sir," Prickett said, backing away to leave Hudson a clear path toward the rigging.

But Jonah caught a glimpse of Prickett's face as Prickett turned aside. His eyes were squinted almost shut, and his teeth were clenched.

He really doesn't want Hudson up in that crow's nest, Jonah thought. *Why? Because there's something about the passageway he doesn't want Hudson to see? Or—because he knows there are papers up there saying he's bad, and he's afraid Hudson will find them?*

Jonah was pretty sure it was the second reason. Should

Jonah call out, *Yo, Dad, look under the canvas when you get up there!*—or something like that, only sounding a little more 1611-ish?

Or would that just make it look like Jonah was the one who'd written and hidden those papers?

Prickett had his eyebrows raised, staring at Jonah.

He knows I'm trying to decide what to do, Jonah thought.

Prickett reminded Jonah of someone. *Who?* Jonah wondered. *How many people do I know who have so many scars and sores and pockmarks? And that long, stringy, thinning hair . . . It has to be someone I've seen traveling through time.*

Then Jonah realized: It wasn't. It was his old friend back home, Billy Rivoli, who liked playing games like Stratego and chess. Physically, Billy didn't look anything like Prickett—Billy had short, thick black hair and braces and was a little bit chubby, because he also liked sitting around eating Oreos all day long. But Billy had always had this way of raising his eyebrows when he was planning to trap Jonah in chess or Stratego. The raised eyebrows always said, *Ha, ha, ha. You will never figure out my brilliant plan. Give up! You've already lost!*

It was almost always true, because the raised eyebrows would make Jonah so mad that he'd do something dumb. And then he really would lose.

Prickett's raised eyebrows made Jonah mad too.

"Father?" Jonah called out to Hudson.

Hudson turned around.

"Yes, son?" he said cautiously.

Jonah caught a glimpse of Prickett's face, though he turned away to hide it.

Prickett was *beaming*. He must have thought Jonah was about to make a huge mistake.

"Just—be careful on those ropes," Jonah said quickly. "They're still a little icy, up by the top."

"Thank you, son," Hudson said.

Jonah couldn't tell from Hudson's voice if Hudson was grateful for the warning, or if he was annoyed that Jonah was acting as if Hudson couldn't even climb a rope without slipping. Jonah knew from his own parents that adults didn't like being treated as if they were too old to do stuff. But Jonah decided he'd done the right thing when he caught another glimpse of Prickett's face.

Prickett was scowling now.

TWENTY-FIVE

The life of the ship went on around Jonah, trapped in his stocks. Katherine went down belowdecks again to look for messages. Hudson went up to the crow's nest and then came back down. Various crew members raised and lowered sails, catching the best winds. Hudson conferred with Prickett, with King, with others. Late in the afternoon Jonah even saw Staffe stride into Hudson's cabin for a brief conversation.

Staffe didn't even look in Jonah's direction on the way out.

Okay. So that hurts my feelings. So what? Jonah told himself. *I've got bigger things to worry about. Like saving all of time. And—Andrea. Will I ever see her again?*

Jonah managed to distract himself for a while just thinking about how pretty Andrea was, with her gray eyes, and her long brown hair, and her fragile air.

She was never as fragile as she looked, Jonah reminded himself.

Again and again, traveling through time, Jonah had discovered that things often weren't as they seemed.

So, here in 1611, am I going to discover that Prickett is the good guy and Staffe is secretly the one who's out to get me? Jonah wondered.

He shook his head. He might be confused about a lot of things, but he refused to believe that the world could be that messed up.

Jonah realized that while he'd been lost in his thoughts, Henry Hudson had come out of his cabin. He looked around, then veered toward Jonah and the stocks.

Around them all the sailors seemed to be carefully looking away—carefully not watching Hudson stop beside his supposed son.

"You know the story of why I ran away to sea, don't you?" Hudson asked. "How I argued with my father about anything and everything, how we couldn't see eye to eye, ever?"

"You've told me that," Jonah said cautiously, because, if he were the real John Hudson, he'd know a story like that, wouldn't he?

"I was just your age," Hudson said. "Your age exactly when I left."

Jonah nodded, because what was he supposed to say to that? *Uh, just how old am I, anyway? Or I kind of doubt it, Pops. If you want to be exactly accurate about how old I am, really, I think you'd have to use negative numbers.*

"And when I got back from my first sea voyage, my father was dead," Hudson said, staring at a point just above Jonah's head. "He died a week after I left, but of course I didn't know that. I spent that whole two years at sea imagining coming home to my father, bringing him treasures, making up for all our fights . . ."

Hudson's voice trailed off. He wouldn't start crying, right there, would he?

"He probably knew you wanted to bring him treasure," Jonah said, a bit awkwardly. "He probably knew you didn't want to fight anymore."

"But what if I did?" Hudson said. "What if the treasure was my way of saying, 'See, I was right all along?' The way boys think . . ."

Oh, no, Jonah thought. *Don't make this about "boys." Don't make this about you and your son!*

Hudson shifted his gaze to meet Jonah's eyes.

He's going to see that I'm not really John Hudson! Jonah thought, panicked. *He's going to see that I'm really some other kid in a mask and a wig and a cape!*

Hudson was almost glaring, his eyes narrowed to slits.

"You volunteered!" he said fiercely. "I didn't force you—I wouldn't have forced you. Not my own son!"

"Are you talking about putting me into the stocks?" Jonah asked, his voice coming out like a yelp in his surprise. "You may not have forced me, but John King sure did! Force was used!"

Hudson looked around. A sailor who was rebraiding a frayed rope nearby bent his head lower, clearly trying to pretend that he hadn't heard a thing.

"I'm talking about yesterday!" Hudson hissed, sotto voce. "When you got us the special map!"

Jonah's eyes sprang open so wide he was afraid he might split the John Hudson mask. He barely stopped himself from saying, *What do you mean, I got us the map? What did I do? I thought you got the map! I thought Second gave it to you! This is crazy! What am I supposed to think now?*

"I—," Jonah began, then stopped, because anything he said would just be like screaming out, *I'm not the real John Hudson! I'm a fake!*

Hudson leaned closer.

"Did you run away? How did you do it? Are they following you?" he whispered.

"I can't talk to you about that right now," Jonah said, which was straight out of one of those guidance assemblies at school, where the counselors played out ridiculous role-plays about being offered drugs or alcohol or dealing with bullies or coping with out-of-control emotions. "I can't talk to you about that right now" was supposed to be an all-purpose answer, what you could use when anything else you could think of was bound to get you into trouble. The entire school had made fun of that saying for weeks afterward—even the teachers had joined in.

But, what do you know? Looks like that saying actually does work when you've traveled through time and people are talking to you about stuff you've got no clue about, Jonah thought.

Because Hudson was backing away and murmuring, "Of course. Of course. Sometimes you show wisdom beyond your years, my son. We'll talk later. After you're out of the stocks."

"Um, you couldn't let me out early, could you?" Jonah asked. "Like, give me time off for good behavior? Or—for showing wisdom?"

Hudson looked around, as if suddenly remembering the sailor with the frayed rope, the other sailors clustered around the ship, everyone who could have heard what Jonah said, even if they'd heard none of the whispers and murmurings.

The sailor with the rope resorted to lopping off the end with an axe. The sound of the axe hitting made Jonah jump.

"Of course I can't let you out early," Hudson said coldly.

"I run a tight ship. You will stay in the stocks until sundown tomorrow—not a minute more, not a minute less."

And there's another thing that's different than it seems, Jonah thought. *Henry Hudson doesn't treat his son the same in private as he does when other people are listening.*

But what did that have to do with the map? And what in the world had the real John Hudson "volunteered" for?

TWENTY-SIX

Hours passed. A crew member Jonah hadn't noticed before brought out a crust of hard bread and a flask of rancid water. Jonah discovered that if he thought about something else—the arrangement of desks in his math class back home, say, or the way Andrea had said good-bye the last time he saw her—he could choke down the food and swallow the water without gagging.

Shortly before dusk Katherine came up on deck and hovered nearby. Jonah waved her over and mouthed the words, *I have to tell you something!* But she shook her head and pointed at all the sailors standing nearby.

Later, she mouthed back. She said something else—maybe *when they're gone?* And then she launched into a long, silent explanation that Jonah couldn't make heads or tails of.

If we ever get out of 1611, Jonah thought, *I am definitely learning how to read lips before I ever travel through time again!*

Katherine disappeared back down the stairs.

Jonah kicked his feet against the wooden deck.

"Tsk, tsk, what a show of bad temper," Prickett said, lurking nearby. "Is your punishment wearing on you?"

Jonah wished he'd looked around a little more before he'd started kicking.

"Oh, no," he said, through gritted teeth. "I'm just stretching my legs." That didn't seem like enough when Prickett was sneering so obnoxiously, so Jonah added, "Really, if you think about it, you *rewarded* me, putting me here. I'm getting out of two days of work."

Prickett fixed him with a level stare.

"Indeed," he said. "I will take that into account the next time I recommend your father punish you."

He turned and followed Katherine down the steps.

That was the awful thing about being in the stocks—people could just walk away, even when you weren't done talking to them.

Jonah resisted the urge to kick the deck again.

The sailors coiled up their ropes, tied down the sails, and retreated belowdecks.

Katherine didn't come back.

The sun vanished over the horizon, and everything

around Jonah grew darker and darker and darker.

Streetlights, Jonah thought, listing things he missed about the twenty-first century. *Flashlights. Even tiny glowing cell phone screens . . .*

The Boy Scout camp he'd gone to back home was supposedly out in the middle of nowhere, but even there he and his friends had been able to see the glow of the nearest suburb on the horizon, every night.

The darkness that would descend on this ship tonight would be complete.

Jonah heard footsteps and saw a candle advancing toward him. It was amazing how much better the sight of that candle made him feel.

"Katherine?" he whispered eagerly into the darkness. He knew he should tell her to blow out the candle, but . . . maybe another minute or two of it would be all right?

"Katherine?" a deep voice repeated. "Is that the name of the girl in that picture you dream about?"

The candle drew nearer, and Jonah saw that Staffe was the one holding it.

"No, no," Jonah muttered, embarrassed. How was he going to explain this one? "She's . . . just someone else I was thinking about. Remembering."

"*Another* girlfriend?" Staffe teased.

"No! My—" Jonah started to say "sister," but then he

remembered that Staffe had been on the same ship with John and Henry Hudson for more than a year. He'd know if the real John Hudson had a sister named Katherine or not. And odds were he didn't.

"Just a relative," Jonah finished weakly.

Jonah couldn't tell if Staffe believed him or not. The man's expression grew thoughtful.

"I see," he murmured. "Thoughts do turn to faraway family on dangerous nights like this one. But—" He held the candle near Jonah's face, and seemed to be looking at him intently. "You weren't thinking you saw this relative on the ship, were you? Thinking you see people and things that aren't really there?"

"Of course not," Jonah said indignantly. "I know what's real and what isn't."

Note to self, Jonah thought. *Don't say anything about how my sister's invisible, and she and I traveled through time to get here, and we'd be okay if we could just get through to someone who's stuck in 1600, and . . .*

"Good," Staffe said, seeming to relax a bit. "Too many people on this ship are having trouble not knowing what's real. Did you hear Wydowse is down below, on the verge of death, and talking half out of his mind?"

He shook his head sorrowfully. Jonah tried to remember which sailor was Wydowse—oh, yeah, the one from the shallop, with the compass.

The one who'd pointed out that the *Discovery* could not possibly have come back for them from the southwest, when it had sailed away from them toward the northeast.

"But I did not come out here just to bring you bad news," Staffe said. "Look."

He pulled a book out of his coat and held it out to Jonah. By squinting, Jonah could just barely make out the title in the dim candlelight: *New Views of the New World*.

That's what it said at the top of the picture of Andrea! Jonah thought excitedly.

"Now *you* stole one of my father's books?" Jonah asked incredulously. "After yelling at me about taking just one page? *And* throwing my paper into the water?"

He was not going to forgive Staffe for that.

"I am no thief," Staffe said sternly. "I got your father's permission to borrow this book, to look at the picture of the natives' kayaks. I suggested that we might want to try building one ourselves, for use in fishing."

Jonah didn't care about kayaks right now.

"I just didn't tell your father I would also be showing the book to you," Staffe said.

Staffe sounded so pleased with himself it annoyed Jonah. Jonah had been trapped in the stocks for most of the day. His knees hurt, his back ached—and now that he thought about it, his stomach ached, too, probably because of the moldy bread and the rancid water. His mind was full of maps that he had supposedly found and rivers that had seemingly appeared out of nowhere . . . and friends who were counting on him, that he was going to let down, because he didn't understand anything that was going on.

"Why would you think I care?" Jonah asked sulkily. "Why would I care about that book when my favorite page is missing?"

"Because," Staffe said, his face glowing in the candle-light, "there's another picture of that girl in here."

TWENTY-SEVEN

"Let me see!" Jonah said, reaching for the book.

He thought Staffe was probably mistaken—how closely had Staffe looked at the picture of Andrea, anyway, before he threw it overboard? But if there was even a chance, Jonah had to look.

Staffe moved the book out of Jonah's reach.

"Careful," he said. "You haven't exactly proved trustworthy with books. You hold the candle. I'll hold the book."

Jonah gritted his teeth and took the candle in his hand as Staffe turned pages.

"I think it was here—nay, a few pages on," he murmured. "Yes, this is it."

He held the book up before Jonah's eyes. The candle illuminated only half the page, so Jonah saw the caption under the picture before he saw the picture itself.

The Death of John White, the caption said.

Jonah gasped.

"It's not her?" Staffe asked sadly.

"No, no, I think it is—let me *see*," Jonah cried, grabbing the book from Staffe's hand.

He tilted the book and the candle, so most of the light landed on the picture.

It did indeed show Andrea, bent over an elderly, white-haired man. Both of them had their eyes closed, but somehow the artist who'd drawn the picture—was it one of their friends? Brendan? Antonio?—had managed to make it clear that Andrea's eyes were closed in sorrow, while the man had abandoned consciousness altogether. The tips of Andrea's braids brushed against his collar, and she seemed to be kissing his forehead.

Kissing him good-bye.

"Careful—the dripping wax," Staffe said.

Jonah tilted the book and the candle the other way around, so the wax rolled harmlessly down to the wooden deck.

"You didn't tell me her grandfather died," Jonah said in a choked voice.

"Are you *crying?*" Staffe asked.

Jonah didn't answer.

"Do you know this girl and her grandfather?" Staffe asked, sounding even more puzzled. "Did you not know of his death before we sailed? Your father has had this book on his shelf the entire journey. Did he not tell you of this man's passing?"

Jonah sniffed.

"It's complicated," he said.

John White—Andrea's grandfather in original time—had been the reason Andrea had wanted to stay in 1600 as Virginia Dare. He'd been the reason Second had been able to use Andrea to manipulate time, the reason Second could *change* time.

And after all that, John White had just died?

"When?" Jonah asked. He moved the candle to illuminate the text below the picture again, so if there was a date, he'd see it.

The type below the caption was tiny and blurry, and said nothing about John White's death.

> John White, governor of the ill-fated Roanoke Colony, reported that rumors of the lost John Cabot map were rampant among sea captains sailing the North American coast. But the natives he encountered in Virginia knew nothing of it, and nothing of the Northwest Passage.

A shiver flowed through Jonah's body that had nothing to do with the cold air blowing across the deck.

"A map!" he whispered. "The Northwest Passage! Then it's all connected? But how? And—who's John Cabot?"

"'John Cabot.'" Staffe repeated the name thoughtfully. "Seems I have heard your father speak that name—have you not?" He pitched his voice a bit lower, and elongated his vowels a bit more, imitating Henry Hudson. "'John Cabot accomplished nothing. 'Tis hard to believe he sailed to any of the places he claimed to have seen. But I—I shall bring back proof! People will know and remember me!'"

Jonah laughed.

"Sounds just like him!" Jonah said. "You're really good at that!"

A look of fear dropped across Staffe's face like a mask.

"I—I'm sorry," he stuttered. "I do not mean to mock the captain. I pray you, tell no one!"

"Hey, I'm in the *stocks*," Jonah said. "Who's going to believe anything I say?"

This didn't seem to comfort Staffe. He snatched the candle back from Jonah and held it out in a circle around them, to see if anyone was nearby.

"Did you just hear something?" Staffe asked.

Wind, Jonah wanted to say. *The ropes thumping against the masts. The current hitting against the ship. The same sounds I've been hearing all day.*

But he knew what Staffe was really asking.

"Relax," Jonah said. "Everyone's either belowdecks or holed up in the captain's cabin. Nobody could have heard y—"

He swallowed the last word, because Staffe's candle illuminated a face right behind him—a face that the light passed through, a face that was almost completely transparent, a face that Staffe didn't see at all.

It was Katherine.

You can't sneak up on people like that! Jonah wanted to yell at her. *I almost jumped out of my skin, and now how am I supposed to explain my reaction to Staffe?*

"What?" Staffe said, in a panicked tone. He swung the candle more widely, even though that made the flame flicker and almost sputter out.

"Nothing," Jonah said. "I just saw a shadow that tricked my eyes for a moment." He tried to shrug, but that was pretty much impossible with his neck trapped in the stocks.

He glared at the spot where he'd seen Katherine's face, even though that whole area was suffused in darkness now, since Staffe had moved the candle.

Katherine tapped Jonah on the shoulder. She stepped

into the new area dimly illuminated by the candle's glow, pointed to Staffe, and made a shoving motion. Then she pointed to her own mouth, pantomimed talking, and then pointed to Jonah.

Back in 1600, Katherine had gotten very annoyed with Jonah once because he didn't instantly understand her improvised sign language. But Jonah was sure that he understood her perfectly this time. She was saying, *Get rid of Staffe! I have to talk to you! Now!*

"Um, could I maybe talk to you about all of this later?" Jonah asked Staffe. "It was really nice of you to show me the book, and I want to look at it again, but—"

"Do you know how hard it was to sneak away?" Staffe asked incredulously. "I had to stay awake until everyone around me was soundly asleep. I—"

"I know!" Jonah interrupted. "I just don't want you to get into trouble because of me! If you get caught out here, and then you're punished because of me—I'd feel terrible."

Staffe stared at Jonah. Jonah decided he hated candlelight after all. It provided just enough illumination that you *thought* you could see, but you could never see enough, no matter how much you strained your eyes. Staffe's face was still mostly in darkness, his scars transformed into deep shadows. Jonah couldn't even begin to tell what the man was thinking.

"I see," Staffe finally said. "How thoughtful of you."

He doesn't believe me, Jonah thought. *He can tell I've got ulterior motives. Now he won't trust me ever again.*

"Thank you for showing me the book," Jonah said.

Staffe shrugged. He took the book back and walked away.

Jonah turned to Katherine as soon as the man was gone.

"This had better be important," Jonah hissed at her.

"It is!" she whispered back, urgently. "Something really awful just happened!"

"Well, what is it?" Jonah asked impatiently.

She put out her hand, bracing herself against the frame of the stocks. Holding on, to counter the rocking of the waves. Or—Jonah looked at her a bit closer—to counter her trembling legs, her shaking hands.

"I started paying attention because I found out who left that letter in the crow's nest," she said. "It was Wydowse. You know, the really old guy? I saw him writing another message."

"That doesn't sound so awful," Jonah said, because she was really starting to freak him out. "Unless—what did the message say?"

"I haven't read it yet," Katherine said. "Because, because

then—" She started gasping for breath, panic and fear battling in her expression.

"Because what?" Jonah asked. "What happened then?"

Katherine took in a huge, desperate breath.

"Prickett killed Wydowse," she said.

TWENTY-EIGHT

"Killed?" Jonah gasped. "He *killed* him? Are you sure?"

Automatically he glanced toward the stairs, because if a murder had just occurred belowdecks, surely there'd be men running up to notify the captain. Surely there'd be sailors screaming, *Put that gun down!* or *Put that sword down!* or *No! Don't kill me, too!*

The stairs were silent and dark and, as far as Jonah could tell in the little bit of light that remained, completely empty. The only sound Jonah could hear from below was the thin edge of a snore.

"Why isn't anyone screaming?" Jonah asked.

Katherine's face twisted in anguish.

"Nobody knows he's dead yet, except me. And Prickett." She pressed her hands over her mouth, then let them slip down. "Oh, Jonah, I should have stopped him, shouldn't I? But I couldn't—I didn't know what was going on until it was over."

"Start at the beginning," Jonah said, which was what Mom always said to Katherine whenever Katherine came home from school in hysterics over some friend being mean to some other friend, or Katherine not getting invited to the biggest party of the year, or something like that. And then Katherine would talk endlessly.

Jonah thought murder was actually something worth saying "Start at the beginning" about.

"I looked all over for more of those notes like we found in the crow's nest," Katherine said. "There were some hidden in a writing desk down below, but they were just about things that happened weeks ago—some guy named Juet being demoted, some other guy named Bylot being promoted above him, the captain making everyone mad."

"Juet—wasn't that one of the people Prickett said he put out on an ice floe? One of the mutineers?" Jonah asked.

Katherine shrugged.

"I guess," she said, sounding hopeless. "How many people do you think Prickett killed today?"

Jonah shook his head. "Don't think about it that way," he said. "Go on."

"So then, while I was standing there, Wydowse hobbled over to the writing desk and sat down. And his handwriting was exactly the same as the writing on the letters in the crow's nest," Katherine said.

In a different mood Jonah would have felt as if he had to say, sarcastically, *Good job, Sherlock, figuring that out!*—just to keep Katherine from acting too proud of her detective skills. But now he only said, carefully, "Okay." He thought for a moment, and then added, "But you didn't just stand there, reading over his shoulder?"

"No," Katherine said. "That was when people started screaming on the deck, and I came up here, and there was that native standing here, talking about how he'd never seen the river before, and then you started talking to him, too—"

"I know, I know, I remember all that," Jonah said impatiently.

Since neither he nor Katherine had a candle or a lamp, Jonah couldn't see anything around them. Still, Jonah couldn't help sweeping his gaze all around the deck, trying to keep an eye out for—what? Prickett bringing Wydowse's body up on deck, to toss him overboard? Some other horror or danger that Jonah couldn't even imagine?

"So then, after that, I went back belowdecks again,

and Wydowse was slumped over his writing, like this."
She pantomimed someone having a stroke or a heart
attack, and falling forward, sprawled across a desktop.

"His face and his arms were covering his papers, and
he'd spilled his ink—I set it upright, because the ink
was getting in his hair," Katherine said. "And I could tell
he'd just collapsed, just then, because there wasn't that
much ink out yet. . . . Jonah, what would you have done
then?"

This question caught Jonah off guard. He'd actually
been thinking, *Whoa. Kind of glad it was Katherine who had
to deal with all that, not me. Makes being stuck in the stocks seem
not so bad.*

"I don't know," Jonah said slowly. "I guess I would
have tried to figure out how to get Wydowse some help.
Without blowing my cover or making people think the
ship was haunted, or anything like that."

"That's what I thought!" Katherine said, hitting him
on the arm in her excitement.

"So what did you do?" Jonah asked.

"Well, there were other people below the deck,
just not right by Wydowse. And the way his desk
was angled—it could have taken hours before anyone
noticed he'd collapsed," Katherine said. "So I stood
right beside him and I made this noise, trying to sound

like an old man in pain. 'Please help me! I—*glug* . . .' I actually had to do that, like, three or four times before anyone noticed."

"Smart," Jonah admitted grudgingly.

"So some of the other sailors came over, and they tucked Wydowse into bed—well, into his hammock," Katherine said. "And one of them suggested giving him some broth, and the others said, 'No, we'll not waste broth on a man who's just going to die anyway'—and it was awful, it was just like JB was talking about back at the beginning, about how they're all being so selfish with their food!"

Is it selfishness, when there's not enough food to go around? Jonah wondered.

"So I was going to get some broth for Wydowse myself, just to serve them right!" Katherine said indignantly. "But—there were always people clustered around, so I couldn't."

"What was Prickett saying?" Jonah asked.

"He wasn't there then," Katherine said. "I came upstairs to ask you what you thought we should do, but there were people all around you, too."

"I would have said, 'Read the papers on the desk!'" Jonah said, shaking his head in disgust.

"Oh, I thought of that," Katherine said. "When they

moved Wydowse to his hammock, I looked right away, but the papers were turned facedown, like he'd just flipped the last one over to write on the back."

"Then you could have picked them up!" Jonah said, barely managing to resist adding an insult like, *What are you, stupid?*

"There were people around, remember?" Katherine asked. "You think they needed to see papers floating through the air?"

Oh, yeah. . . .

Jonah was glad he'd resisted calling his sister stupid.

"But I kept waiting and waiting for the right moment," Katherine said. "Because people were starting to drift away—it's not like any of them could do anything to help Wydowse. But then he started talking."

"Talking?" Jonah repeated.

"Yeah, like, babbling," Katherine said. "He kept saying, 'It makes no sense,' and 'John Cabot's map couldn't have survived out here for more than a hundred years,' and—"

"Wait—he was talking about John Cabot's map?" Jonah interrupted. "But—that was in the book, with the picture of Andrea and John White!"

"It was?" Katherine asked. "I don't remember seeing—"

"Not the original picture," Jonah said. "The one Staffe showed me . . . oh, finish your story, and then I'll tell mine."

Katherine looked puzzled, but shook her head and went back to talking.

"Someone must have gone to get Prickett, because he came in and said, 'Let's leave the poor man in peace,'" she said. "And then—" Katherine's voice turned hollow, as if she had to force herself to continue. "Then Prickett pretended to leave with everyone else. I saw him walk out! Then all the lights went out belowdecks, and Wydowse did seem to settle down. He was just, like, whimpering, every few minutes. And I was going to just grab the papers and tiptoe away, but then I heard Prickett's voice, whispering to Wydowse, 'I can't have you talking like that. You're too smart. You've guessed too much.'"

She spoke the same way Prickett must have: in a low voice, with a threatening growl that no one could have heard more than a few feet away. She was too good at the imitation. Jonah started shivering, and couldn't stop.

"And then Prickett must have suffocated Wydowse, or poisoned him, or something," Katherine said.

"But you didn't *see* what he did?" Jonah asked.

"It was pitch-black!" Katherine said. "I could barely make out shadows! But Prickett stood over Wydowse for a long time, and then I heard him tiptoeing away, and right away I went over to see why Wydowse wasn't talking anymore at all. And, and—"

"You've seen dead bodies before," Jonah said, and he meant it in a comforting way.

"But I'd never touched one!" Katherine protested. "I could *feel* his skin getting cold!"

Jonah did not want to dwell on this.

"Okay, okay, Katherine," he said in his most soothing voice. "I know this is really awful, but you have to go back down there and get those papers from the desk. They're probably, like, evidence against Prickett, and—"

"I'm not stupid," Katherine said. "I didn't panic or anything! I picked up those papers on my way out of the room! Here!"

She thrust something into Jonah's hand. For a moment Jonah needed to steady himself: *They're just papers. Okay, they were written by a man who was murdered a few minutes ago, but all you're holding is paper. You didn't have to touch the dead guy. You just need to think clearly. . . .*

"Light," he said out loud, trying to sound normal. "We're going to need a candle or a lantern and, oh, I guess, something to light it with—"

"Or perhaps something to burn those with?" a deep voice said.

And a second later Jonah wasn't holding any papers. They'd been snatched straight from his hand. .

TWENTY-NINE

"No!" Jonah cried. Instantly a hand clapped across his mouth. Jonah tried to bite down on the fingers, but then there was an arm clutching his head.

And squeezing.

"You make another sound, and I can dream up worse punishments than the stocks," the voice whispered in his ear.

Jonah was almost certain it was Prickett, but in the darkness he was confused. He heard something different in the voice than he'd heard looking into the man's face.

Jonah heard a scratching noise—flint, perhaps?—then a candle sparked to life, enclosed in a metal holder that looked strangely familiar.

Oh, yeah, Jonah thought. *It looks like the twin to our Elucidator.*

The candle flared, and Jonah could see Prickett's scarred, weather-beaten face. He lost track of whatever he'd thought he heard in Prickett's voice before.

"Silence. Agreed?" Prickett said.

Behind Prickett, Jonah could see Katherine, pointing to her mouth, open wide, then flaring her hands out— then raising them, questioningly. This time Jonah could understand exactly what she was saying: *I could scream, right now, and he couldn't stop me! He couldn't even see me! Should I scream or not?*

Jonah shook his head, ever so slightly.

"Silence," he whispered in agreement.

Katherine, you're our secret weapon, he thought at his sister, hoping she could figure that out, too. *Don't give away that you're here unless you really need to. Let's figure out what's going on first.*

Prickett pulled his hand back, though he kept it cupped, ready to slap over Jonah's mouth again at any moment if he had to.

"Smart boy," Prickett said. "You know no one's going to believe some crazy story told by a boy in the stocks. Certainly not when he maligns the man who saved the ship's captain from almost-certain death this morning."

He was holding the papers slightly off to the side. Jonah saw Katherine reach for them, but it was uncanny—

Prickett chose that exact moment to move them over in front of his face.

"Now, Wydowse—everyone might believe Wydowse," Prickett mused, looking down at the papers. "As long as his writing's more lucid than his talking's been, these past few hours."

"You—," Jonah began, and caught himself. What he'd wanted to do was shout, *You killed him!* But even if he hadn't just agreed to be silent, it didn't seem like a good idea to remind Prickett he was capable of murder. Not when the deck was so dark and deserted. Not when Jonah was trapped in the stocks.

Jonah remembered the axe the sailor with the rope had left by the mast.

It would be so easy for Prickett to kill me, Jonah thought, hiding a shiver. *And Katherine couldn't stop him. She couldn't even grab the papers away from him.*

Prickett was still studying the papers.

"Tsk, tsk," he said. "Such awful accusations Wydowse makes. . . ." He looked up again at Jonah. "And how is it that you got those papers, when you've been trapped in the stocks all day? Who gave them to you?"

Jonah opened his mouth. Did he want to lie, and cast blame on someone who'd done nothing? Did he want to try to clear someone's name? Even if he said,

It wasn't Staffe! that would just make it sound as if Staffe were guilty.

"Never mind. I wouldn't expect a reprobate like you to answer me honestly," Prickett said. "You got them from *someone*. I'll find him out, whoever he is."

Jonah glared at Prickett. But in the dim candlelight Prickett probably couldn't even see his face.

"My informants tell me that Wydowse left hidden testimony all over the ship," Prickett continued in a leisurely tone. "The other ship's boy, Nicholas Symmes—poor thing, like so many others on this ship he can't even read—he admitted that he hid papers up in the top for Wydowse."

Numbly, Jonah remembered that "top" was what people on the ship called the crow's nest.

Prickett kept talking.

"Symmes didn't even know what he was hiding. But to truly silence Wydowse, perhaps I should destroy those papers when I destroy these? Don't you agree?" Prickett leered triumphantly at Jonah. "Oh, that's right—I've silenced you as well."

The leer turned into a smirk, as Prickett's eyebrows darted upward.

That expression—he looks like somebody, and it's not Billy Rivoli back home, Jonah thought.

It was crazy, thinking about how Prickett looked at a time like this.

"Don't!" Jonah choked out. "You can't—"

"What? Are you going to stop me?" Prickett asked.

He laughed and whirled around, heading toward the rigging that led to the crow's nest.

"I'll stop him!" Katherine hissed, racing behind him.

"No, Katherine—not alone! Set me free! I'm coming with you!" Jonah called after her.

For a moment Jonah thought Katherine would ignore him. She kept running. But then she half turned in the darkness.

"People will know," she said, still poised to run. "I can't get you out without leaving evidence—"

"That doesn't matter!" Jonah hissed. "Quick! The axe!"

Katherine looked around. There was so little light—would she have to waste a lot of time groping around just trying to find the axe? No—she had it. She picked it up and swung it at the lock holding the stocks together. Jonah heard the wood splintering.

"Didn't quite work . . . one more time," Katherine whispered.

Prickett's candle was so far away now that Jonah couldn't even see Katherine swinging the axe. It was too dark. But he felt the vibration in the wood when the axe hit. And then Katherine was lifting the top part of the stocks off his neck and wrists.

"Come *on!*" Katherine whispered.

Both of them took off running.

THIRTY

Jonah's legs were stiff after spending so many hours in the stocks. Katherine reached the bottom of the rigging far ahead of him.

"Wait!" he called to her. "We'll go up together!"

"But Prickett's getting away!" Katherine called over her shoulder, as she started climbing.

She was right. They could see Prickett's progress easily, since he was carrying the candle. He was several yards above them, and the light kept swinging steadily upward.

Is he holding it in his teeth? Jonah wondered. *Does he have it tied to his arm somehow?*

Jonah was annoyed with his brain, that it would worry about such unnecessary details at a time like this. What he really needed to do was concentrate on bringing his sore muscles back to life, coordinating his arms and legs into top climbing form. He needed to go fast, to catch up with Katherine, to catch up with Prickett.

He grabbed the bottom of the rigging with his right hand and tried to pull himself up. His arms wobbled.

Okay, he thought. *Spending the whole day in the stocks made my arm muscles feel terrible too.*

He shook out his arms and tried again. It didn't help that the rigging was so cold and wet. He'd warned Henry Hudson about the ropes being icy hours ago, when the sun was still up. Probably they really were by now.

Jonah's fingers turned numb so quickly that he couldn't tell if there was ice on the ropes or not.

Slow and steady, his brain advised him. *You start trying to go fast, you'll fall.*

How was it that Prickett wasn't falling, going so fast, so far ahead?

Jonah's mind supplied him with an image of the man plummeting straight down to the deck, screaming all the way.

And then Jonah froze, because his mind started seeing himself fall, rather than Prickett.

If I get much higher—it'd be high enough to kill me when I hit the deck, Jonah thought.

But he had to stop Prickett from burning those papers!

Jonah's muscles still refused to move. Above him Prickett

and Katherine were getting farther and farther ahead.

So I'm going to leave Katherine to deal with a murderer all by herself? Jonah wondered.

That got his arms and legs working again. His fingers were still numb, his muscles were still stiff, but he fell into a rhythm. He picked up speed. He lost track of how much farther it was to the crow's nest. In some ways it was easier to climb in the darkness—he couldn't see the deck receding below him. All he had to focus on was the light bobbing above him. He was actually closing in on it now. He was closing in on—

He ran into Katherine's foot.

"Sorry," he whispered.

"Shh," she whispered back. "We're close enough he could hear us."

Not with the wind, Jonah thought. Because it was eerie—Jonah could barely feel the wind around him, but he could hear it shrieking like a horrible storm. Maybe it was just because of the altitude they'd reached.

No, don't think that, Jonah told himself.

He heard a thump above them, and the light stopped rising.

"He's in the crow's nest now!" Jonah hissed at Katherine. "Go grab those papers from him—try to do it so he just thinks they blew away in the wind!"

Katherine started climbing faster, closer and closer to Prickett and the crow's nest and the light. Prickett had hung the candleholder on some sort of hook high on the mast, so the light shone down through the gaps in the crow's nest. It glowed right through Katherine.

Good thing she's translucent, Jonah thought. *Otherwise I wouldn't be able to see a thing.*

He wanted to call out some kind of warning to his sister—something like, *Don't let him see you!*—but that was ridiculous, because of course she was completely invisible to Prickett. He and everyone else who truly belonged in 1611 had looked straight through her hundreds of times that day.

"Careful," Jonah whispered anyway.

Prickett chose that moment to lean out slightly over the railing of the crow's nest, looking down. But of course he couldn't have heard Jonah, because of the wind; he couldn't see Jonah, because the light was so dim.

Jonah stopped climbing.

I'll only go on up to the crow's nest if Katherine needs me, he thought. *If she can't get the papers, can't make it look like they've flown off into the wind . . .*

Katherine was at the top of the rigging now, at the place where she'd have to flip over into the crow's nest.

Then grab the papers; then hide them in your clothes; then start climbing back down, Jonah thought, as if he could direct his sister's actions by telepathy.

He was so focused on what she was going to do, what was supposed to happen, that he almost couldn't make sense of what his eyes told him was happening right that moment:

Katherine's hand slipped.

She teetered over backward, and Jonah actually screamed, "No! Grab on!" Because nothing else mattered in that moment but Katherine being safe, Katherine holding on, Katherine not falling. . . .

No! No! No! Jonah's brain screamed.

Because she *was* falling. She tried to get her grip again. But both her hands slid off the ropes, slid off the railing. Her feet slipped too, and then she was tumbling down, the flickering candlelight making everything seem as if it were happening in slow motion. But in a second it would speed up, she would plunge into the darkness below, and—

Prickett reached out and grabbed Katherine by the wrist. Then he yanked her over into the crow's nest.

THIRTY-ONE

Jonah's brain stopped working.

What he'd just seen was impossible. Prickett couldn't have grabbed Katherine and rescued her. He couldn't have *seen* her to rescue her, because Katherine was completely invisible to everyone but time travelers. And Prickett wasn't a time traveler; he belonged in 1611. He looked just as starved and scarred and scurvy-ridden as everyone else on the ship; everyone knew him and acted as if he'd been there all along.

Of course, Jonah also looked just as starved and scarred and scurvy-ridden as everyone else on the ship; everyone recognized him as John Hudson and acted as if he'd been there all along.

If Jonah was a time traveler disguised as a 1611 boy, couldn't Prickett be a time traveler disguised as a 1611 man?

How else could he have seen Katherine to rescue her?

Jonah realized his brain was working, after all. It was just working slowly.

Even as he clung to the rigging, all but paralyzed in place, his brain lurched on to the next question:

If Prickett was actually a time traveler, not a 1611 sailor, who was he for real? Was he somebody Jonah knew?

Prickett leaned out over the railing.

"You might as well climb on up here too, Jonah," he called out softly.

So, Jonah thought. *Whether or not I know him, he knows me.*

He had to peel his numb fingers from the rope he'd been clinging to.

Maybe I should be climbing down—running away, Jonah thought. *Whoever he is, Prickett murdered Wydowse.*

But Prickett had also rescued Katherine.

And—he still had Katherine in the crow's nest with him.

Jonah took a deep breath and started climbing up. He reached the crow's nest just as Katherine was blinking up at Prickett and murmuring, "If that's really you, JB, I'm going to be so mad that you didn't tell us you were on the ship with us this whole time."

Prickett shook his head.

"You know JB's stuck in the past," he said. "He can't even talk to you."

"Hadley?" Jonah guessed, stepping gingerly over the railing. "Hadley Correo?"

Hadley was another time traveler who'd worked with JB and had helped them out on one of their previous trips through time, back in the 1400s. That time he'd kept his identity secret until a particularly dangerous moment. If this was Hadley, Jonah wished he'd revealed himself a lot sooner. But it would still be so good to see him, to know that someone who knew a lot about time was there to help them.

Prickett practically pouted.

"Wrong again," he said. "I'm insulted that you haven't figured this out already. Who's responsible for you being in 1611 in the first place?"

"JB," Katherine and Jonah said, almost simultaneously.

"No, no, no," Prickett said, truly sounding annoyed now. "Who's *really* responsible? JB would never have been so reckless if I hadn't forced his hand, forced history to change, forced everyone to count on two inexperienced children to save all of time. . . ."

Jonah clutched the railing behind him. He didn't trust the way the crow's nest lurched about, dipping and tilting with the whim of the waves so far below him. He didn't trust the way the wind shrieked, seeming to promise tornadoes, hurricanes, blizzards—dangers Jonah could only imagine.

But most of all Jonah didn't trust the man standing before him.

"Second?" he whispered.

THIRTY-TWO

Jonah half expected Second to rip off his Abacuk Prickett costume, revealing his true self. Jonah had seen the man only briefly when they'd first met, back in 1600—and Jonah had been in shock then, trying to comprehend massive changes in time. But Jonah still remembered Second's pasty-white skin, which looked as though he'd hardly ever spent a moment outdoors. He remembered Second's sticking-out-all-over-the-place blond hair; his half-tucked shirt; the smug, smirking tone that hung over Second's every word.

That's why Prickett sounded different to me when I couldn't see his face, Jonah thought. Even when Second was using Prickett's voice, he still sounded like he was smirking. And that one time I did catch a bit of his smug expression. . . .

Second's appearance didn't change at all—he still

looked like the scarred, starving, sickly Abacuk Prickett, his skin as weather-beaten as an old shoe.

"So what are you doing here?" Jonah asked accusingly. "What are you *trying* to do?"

"For the last fifteen or twenty minutes I've been trying to lure the two of you up to this crow's nest," Second said. "I'd say I succeeded."

Katherine sprang up and grabbed the railing, clutching it every bit as desperately as Jonah was.

"Now, now," Second said. "I just saved your life. Do you think I would have done that if my intent was to harm you?"

"You killed Wydowse," Katherine accused, even as Jonah shook his head frantically at her.

Don't make him mad! Jonah thought at his sister. *Let's get down from here; let's get somewhere safe. Then we can start throwing out the accusations!*

But Second only began thoughtfully tapping his chin.

"*Did* I kill Wydowse?" he asked, as if it were merely an academic question. "Or did he just die on his own at a very convenient time? How will you ever know? He was desperately ill. That time he spent in the shallop, and standing on the deck watching Jonah being put in the stocks, and even sitting at his desk writing so feverishly . . . all of that had to have taken its toll on him."

"You had a motive," Katherine insisted. "The things he was writing about you—about Prickett, I mean . . ."

Second laughed and almost playfully hit Katherine on the head with the rolled-up papers from Wydowse's desk.

"Actually, these papers are more incriminating toward my goals than toward Prickett's character," Second said. "Wydowse was a scientist, skilled at observation. Even near death he could see the logical inconsistencies around him. And he wanted so badly to record his observations, in hopes that someone could make sense of them in the future. But, alas, his writings are too dangerous to stay on this ship."

Second sounded so careless and offhand, Jonah didn't anticipate what happened next: Second ripped the papers in half.

Both Jonah and Katherine sprang at him, a dangerous motion in the crowded crow's nest.

If he holds his hands up in the air, we'll have to grab the papers before he throws them out into the water, Jonah thought. *We'll have to jump. But we can't jump too high or too far, or we'll all fall. . . .*

But Second didn't try to keep the ripped papers away from Jonah and Katherine. Instead he handed them right to them—the top half to Katherine, the bottom to Jonah.

In his astonishment Jonah almost dropped his half.

"You wanted those papers so badly—don't you know

what to do with them?" Second asked sardonically. "What if I change my mind and try to take them back?"

Quickly Jonah tucked his half into his cloak. Then he decided that wasn't good enough, and he shoved them between his shirt and his skin instead. Katherine stuffed hers into her jeans pocket.

Second laughed.

"Don't worry—I'm not taking them back," he said, shaking his head. "I probably need you to have those."

Now, what did that mean? Jonah wondered.

He felt a little like some helpless prey, hypnotized by a snake's gaze.

Don't let Second keep control of the conversation, Jonah told himself. *Throw him off. Surprise him into revealing more than he intends.*

But Second was the champion of predictions. Before he'd betrayed JB, Second had been a projectionist, someone who always knew what to expect. Nothing surprised him.

Jonah tried anyway.

"So why did you want us up here?" he asked abruptly. "What's the point?"

This earned another laugh from Second.

"Now you're thinking!" he chortled. "Don't ask about the past, ask about *now,* the only moment we have any control over. Isn't that right? Isn't that what people always said about time before they learned they could go back and change the past after all?"

Jonah remembered that back in 1600, Second had seemed a little off, a little too happy.

A little crazy.

But he still outsmarted us, Jonah thought. *He outsmarted JB. Sometimes craziness works.*

"Have you noticed what a small ship this is?" Second asked. "How difficult it is to find a space where three people can talk in secret, without being overheard? Without being seen?" He glanced at Katherine. "The second part of that is not such a problem for you, my dear, but for Jonah and me . . ." He shook his head. "There have been enough events this day to strain credulity, even among a bunch of superstitious, feverish, starving sailors. Up here I can cover our conversation with the sound of a fake wind."

Jonah realized that that was the reason the wind sounded so fierce when he could hardly feel it at all.

Second was still talking.

"Under the circumstances the crew would be completely undone if they heard a female voice, coming from nowhere," he said. "Or the sight of sworn enemies holding a cozy tête-à-tête . . ."

Jonah forced himself to try to keep up.

"Wait a minute," he said. "You're saying you and me—er,

Abacuk Prickett and John Hudson—we're sworn enemies?"

"Oh, we weren't before today," Second said. "John Hudson was kind of a goody-goody, the peacemaker on the ship, even though *some* of the crew hated him just because of his father. But today it became necessary for me to totally discredit you, just in case you started to spout off, accusing me of, oh, I don't know—messing with time, maybe? Releasing a ripple of bizarre changes from 1600? Being an impostor?"

Second grinned as if this were all a joke.

"And, too, I had to get you into those stocks," he went on. "You were inept enough climbing up to the crow's nest this morning. What if somebody had asked you to raise the mizzen sail? Or tie off the halyard? Climb out on the bowsprit? You would have been hopeless. You might have gotten hurt. You definitely would have blown your cover as John Hudson."

"So you were protecting me, putting me in the stocks?" Jonah asked faintly.

"Protecting you, protecting time—today it was all the same," Second said with a shrug.

"You still care about time?" Katherine asked, sounding startled. "After everything you've done to ruin it—"

"Yes, well, it turns out I have to care," Second said. "It's a technicality, really, some little things that have to be fixed."

Jonah felt his knees go weak with relief.

"You will fix time, then," he said. "You're back on JB's team. On our side."

"Um, no," Second said. "Sorry. It's more like—you have to join my team. You're going to save time, and me."

"What if we don't want to?" Katherine asked. "You're a murderer!"

"Oh, that again," Second said, waving the accusation away as if it meant nothing. "I'm afraid you don't have much of a choice. If you don't do what I want, the paradoxes bury us all."

"*Bury* us?" Jonah repeated in a faint voice.

"Perhaps an unfortunate choice of words—the two of you have such a morbid outlook this evening!" Second said. "I wish I could break this to you a little more subtly, but time is growing short. Put simply, you *have* to help me."

"What happens if we don't?" Katherine challenged.

"We all die—everyone and everything," Second said. His smirk had vanished; his voice was completely serious. "If you don't help me, all of time ends in 1611."

THIRTY-THREE

Jonah backed up against the railing of the crow's nest again, his knees wobbly. He needed *something* to steady him.

It can't be that bad, Jonah thought.

One thing they'd discovered about Second back in 1600 was that even when he told the truth, he sometimes left out important details. What was Second *not* telling them? And how could they get Second to reveal everything?

Katherine went for the blunt approach.

"Why should we believe you?" she asked. "That doesn't even make sense. I mean, how could I be standing here if time ends in 1611? It's going to be, like, almost four hundred years before I'm even born!"

"Oh, good. You're catching on quickly," Second said. "That's one of the paradoxes. Given the direction time is going now, it's become impossible for you to ever exist. Or Jonah. Or me. So everything we've done here, everything we've caused to happen—it's all impossible too. So, poof!" He gestured wildly, mimicking an explosion. "Time could collapse. Everything could end." He put one hand over his heart and finished melodramatically: "Good-bye, cruel world."

"Shouldn't you have thought of that before?" Jonah grumbled.

"Now, now," Second scolded. "I was sure there'd be a way out. I was just as hopeful as Henry Hudson, sailing into the dead-end James Bay, believing so strongly that he'd find a passage to China. . . ."

"But there *wasn't* one for Hudson," Katherine protested. "The Northwest Passage didn't exist. And he was supposed to disappear in a rowboat in the ice!"

"Not anymore," Second said. "Hudson's back with his ship. And—what do you think we're sailing through right now?"

Jonah stared at him.

Second-disguised-as-Prickett brought the ship back to Hudson, Jonah thought. *So for the other changes . . .*

"You dug the Northwest Passage yourself," Jonah said, suddenly understanding. "That's why that native said he'd never seen this river before. You just created it.

You're probably making everything up as we go along!"

"How?" Katherine asked faintly.

"Robotic diggers from the future—believe me, it was *very* complicated working all this out," Second said.

"But why bother?" Katherine asked. "Who cares?"

Second scowled at her.

"Do you know how much time explorers spent searching for the Northwest Passage?" Second asked. "John Cabot, 1497; Samuel Champlain, 1604 to 1607; Hudson, Davis, Baffin . . . Even when Thomas Jefferson sent Lewis and Clark west in 1803, he was hoping they'd come back with news of a river route that stretched all the way to the West Coast. If Europeans had found such a route before they'd even seen much of North America, would they have swarmed to this continent even faster? Or would they have said, 'The Americas? Who cares? Let's just get to China and back as fast as we can!' Would they have left the Native Americans alone? Would the ties between Europe and China and Japan have developed centuries sooner? Would India's role in history change? The possibilities are so fascinating to contemplate! This is so much fun!"

He was practically clapping his hands.

"But is that 'fun' worth threatening all of time?" Jonah asked. "Killing everybody?"

"No, no, you weren't listening closely enough," Second

said, shaking his head. "You're going to stop that from happening. Everything's going to be fine."

Jonah looked at Katherine. Even with his trembling legs and his wobbly muscles, he wished they could just beat up Second and be done with it, or shove him away and scramble down the rigging—or do something else that required only physical strength and effort. It was so much harder to stand here and listen to Second and try to sort out the truth from his half-truths and manipulations.

He's not really saying anything different than JB did, that everything depends on me and Katherine, Jonah thought. *But how could JB have wanted us to side with Second?*

Katherine looked like she was going to throw up. Jonah felt the nervous tremors spread to his own stomach.

"I'm not saying we're agreeing to help you," Jonah said cautiously. "But—what do you want us to do?"

"Go back in time," Second said.

"Back to live out more of 1600?" Jonah asked hopefully. "Back to Andrea?"

"*No,* lover boy," Second said, rolling his eyes. "Not such a distant trip."

"But you did promise," Katherine joined in. "Back before we arrived in 1611, you said if we fixed this time period, we could rescue Andrea and JB and Brendan and Antonio—"

"But you haven't fixed this time period yet, have you?" Second asked through gritted teeth. "Don't get so far ahead of yourself. One thing at a time. All I'm asking is for you to go back a little ways in time—back to this morning."

"You mean—back to a moment this morning before we originally landed on the ship?" Jonah asked. "Because we know nobody can live through the same time period more than once."

This had actually struck him as a very comforting rule, the first time he'd heard it. If no one got more than one shot at any one moment, that meant that none of his enemies could keep coming back again and again to the same point in time to attack him all at once.

It would be confusing enough to have his five a.m. happen after he'd lived through the entire rest of the day.

"You think nobody can live through the same time period more than once?" Second asked. "Did JB tell you that?"

"Yes . . . er, no, I guess it was Angela, back home, when we first found out about time travel," Katherine said. "But she'd heard it from JB."

"Ah," Second said. "Well. That *is* what they teach in Time Travel 101." He leaned over and lifted the candleholder from its hook. "But me—I'm in the advanced class. The one nobody else knew existed."

The smirk was back.

Jonah remembered what JB had said when they'd first arrived in 1611, when Jonah and Katherine were still lying on the icy deck, suffering from timesickness: *We didn't know what we were doing. . . . We made even more mistakes than I thought. . . . What we thought about time itself—a lot of that was wrong. . . . Things that don't show up until you've made mistake upon mistake upon mistake . . .*

"*You* changed the rules of time, then," Jonah said. "You re-created them."

"Not exactly," Second said, with fake modesty. "For once you give me too much credit."

"But if we can go back—why don't we go back and fix 1600?" Katherine said, already thinking ahead. "That way we could avoid this whole mess."

She waved her hand toward the darkness beyond the crow's nest, but Jonah knew she meant the river that wasn't supposed to exist, the stocks she'd taken an axe to down below, the dead man lying in his hammock in the hold.

And the mutineers who were left on an ice floe, when it was the captain and those faithful to him who were supposed to die? Jonah wondered.

"You can't go back to 1600," Second said impatiently. "You can only go back and relive a moment where time is unraveling. Where everything is falling apart."

"You're really making this sound appealing," Jonah muttered.

He looked down and saw that his knuckles had turned white where he'd been gripping the railing so hard, for so long.

"I see that I will have to give some explanation," Second said with a sigh. "What do the two of you know about physics?"

"Nothing," Jonah said flatly.

"Um—black holes?" Second tried again.

"They're out in space and scary," Katherine said. "They suck everything into them, and never let anything out."

"Not even light," Jonah added. The darkness beyond the crow's nest was really starting to bother him.

Second sighed again.

"I suppose that will do as a basic explanation," he said. "I bring them up because things happen near a black hole that would seem to defy the rules of physics as they were understood before black holes were discovered. In the same way, in a spot where time is unraveling—"

"You're saying that makes the rules of time different?" Katherine asked.

Second nodded.

"And nobody knew, because nobody unraveled time before," Jonah said. "Not before you. It's your fault."

Second twisted his expression in a way that could have been called a pout if he'd been a little kid.

"You're always so determined to see the negatives," he complained. "Someday my accomplishments will go down in history. I guarantee it."

"That's if history still exists when you're done with it," Jonah muttered.

"It will, it will—shall we proceed?" Second asked, lifting the candleholder from the hook on the mast. He seemed to be looking closely at . . . Was that a digital clock on the side of the candleholder?

Katherine gasped.

"Yours is an Elucidator too," she said.

Jonah was watching Second's face. His habitual smirk had returned.

"And *your* Elucidator still works," Jonah said. "Unlike ours."

"You think so?" Second practically taunted.

Katherine grabbed his arm.

"Let us talk to JB before we do anything else," she pleaded. She glanced at Jonah. "And to Andrea."

Second shook his arm out of Katherine's grasp.

"Who do you think is in charge here?" he asked. "We don't need another mutiny on this ship. I have all the power here. I'm in control."

"No—you just said you need us to help you," Jonah said. "You need us on your side. To save all of time. And all your plans—"

"You'll help me, whether you want to or not," Second said.

He had his head bent over the Elucidator, punching in commands. Jonah saw that they didn't have much more time. He did the only thing he could think of to stall: He yanked his cloak off and threw it toward Second.

Jonah's goal was to have the cloak settle over Second's head and shoulders, snuffing out the candle and keeping him from finishing his commands. Then maybe Jonah or Katherine could grab the Elucidator; they could scramble down the rigging with it; they could . . .

It didn't matter that Jonah couldn't figure out what they would do then. Because the ship lurched violently to the right just as Jonah tossed his cloak. It missed Second entirely and dropped over the edge of the crow's nest, plunging down toward the deck.

"Interesting choice of weapon," Second murmured, completely nonplussed. "It will be even more interesting to see what you do next."

Katherine and Jonah both lunged toward Second, their hands outstretched, reaching for his Elucidator. But he was already stabbing his finger at the Elucidator with a disturbing finality.

"What a fascinating experiment!" he crowed. "I can't wait to see what you choose!"

Katherine and Jonah were on the verge of tackling Second—and then he vanished.

No, Jonah corrected himself. *We vanished. Katherine and me.*

He could no longer see the crow's nest, the railing or the battered rigging. He couldn't have said if they were speeding through Outer Time or not, because everything happened so quickly.

Second said we'd go back to earlier today, Jonah thought, and even his thoughts seemed chopped up and rushed. *We'll have another chance to choose . . . something. . . .*

He felt a cloak around his shoulders again. *Of course, I had the cloak on earlier today.* But this was a clue—he wouldn't get a chance to choose again whether or not to impersonate John Hudson. That decision had already been made.

Now Jonah could feel hard wood pressing against his spine. He'd stopped moving backward through time. He'd arrived . . . somewhere. He realized that he'd had his eyes squeezed shut, in a panic, and he forced himself to open them.

He expected to see the deck of the ship below him,

the early-morning glow of sunrise starting to cut through the fog, the mutiny beginning around him.

Please let this be after *that sailor hit me over the head with a club,* Jonah thought.

His eyes came into focus almost instantaneously—timesickness was evidently nearly nonexistent when you traveled less than twenty-four hours back in time.

He wasn't on the deck of the ship. He didn't have to worry about the sailor with the club.

He and Katherine were back in the shallop, all their choices in the mutiny behind them.

THIRTY-FOUR

"What?" Jonah actually said out loud. "No!"

Nobody else in the shallop looked at him oddly. Maybe "What? No!" was an appropriate thing to say right at this moment. Actually, nobody was looking in his direction at all. They were all staring down toward the other end of the boat—toward the severed end of a rope.

He realized he and Katherine had arrived just as the shallop was cut adrift from the *Discovery*.

Another collection of possible choices eliminated, Jonah thought. *I can't scramble back up the rope, back onto the deck of the ship, to fight against all the mutineers.*

The wind caught the *Discovery*'s sails, and the ship sped away. Jonah couldn't get back to the ship now unless he wanted to jump into the water, struggle through the ice floes—and probably freeze or drown in the process.

And this is already past the point when we last heard JB's voice on our Elucidator, Jonah thought, still trying to figure out what he could possibly do.

He felt a hand against his chest.

"Let me read your half of Wydowse's letter," Katherine hissed in his ear. "Now, while nobody's looking."

Jonah wasn't sure it would still be there—what were the rules for objects transferred backward through time, perhaps even duplicated in time? What happened to those rules when time itself was unraveling? Then he stopped wondered about theoretical issues, because he was too busy trying to figure out how he could keep Katherine from making it look as if a torn sheet of paper were floating through midair.

"I'll get it," he whispered back.

He reached into his shirt and curled his fingers around the paper he found inside.

Okay, so we brought the paper with us, he thought. *So that means . . .*

He lost track of his thoughts, because several people gasped just then. Had they seen the paper in his hand? Had they figured out that, technically speaking, it was a letter from the future, from a man who was going to die in less than twenty-four hours?

No, they were gasping because they'd just seen the huge ice floe floating toward them—the ice that, the last time around, Jonah had feared would sink the shallop.

Jonah slipped the paper onto the seat beside him, hoping no one could see it but Katherine. He remembered that the last time, this was the moment when he'd yelled out, *JB! Get us out of here! Now!*

Should he yell that again? Was that something that needed to be repeated, or something that needed to be changed?

He remembered that his yell had led to Henry Hudson being suspicious of him, and Staffe standing up for him, saying that he was actually praying.

Maybe Jonah should just pray to begin with, and not make Staffe have to lie?

"Please, God!" Jonah screamed. "Help us!"

It felt good to yell that.

"The Lord helps those who help themselves," Staffe called over to him from the opposite side of the shallop.

At the same time Hudson cried out, "Raise *our* sails! Row toward starboard!"

Jonah remembered that the last time around Hudson's cry had been followed very quickly by a hand slamming against the side of his head, and Hudson growling at him, *I said, row!*

This time Jonah decided to avoid getting hit.

He grabbed for an oar. John King, on the other side of the shallop, was barely a split second ahead of Jonah beginning to paddle. And Hudson and Staffe set up sails in the middle of the boat.

Katherine did not help Jonah row this time. She kept her head bent over the papers hidden on the seat beside Jonah.

The wind caught the sails, and the shallop lurched to the left, narrowly edging past the ice.

Jonah stopped rowing.

"I *am* an excellent captain!" Henry Hudson screamed out into the fog. "You had no right to banish me!"

Just as before, during the time that they'd spent avoiding the ice, the larger ship had disappeared. Once again Hudson's screams echoed off nothing but ice. Jonah was certain that no one from the *Discovery* would be able to hear.

Jonah remembered that this was the moment the last time when Hudson had hit him for calling out to JB. Automatically he cringed down in his seat, ready to avoid a blow.

None came. Instead Hudson just looked at him, a puzzled squint traveling across his face.

"Was it all a trick? A lie? A prank?" he asked Jonah,

speaking so softly that few others in the shallop would have been likely to hear him. "Were you toying with your father's dearest hopes?"

Okay, that was new. What did he mean?

"I—I wouldn't do that," Jonah protested. "I support your dearest hopes. If they're possible."

Wouldn't the real John Hudson have said something like that?

For a moment Jonah thought that Hudson really would hit him. Staffe edged closer, as if ready to protect him.

But Hudson fell back, still squinting.

"The map," he murmured dazedly. "The map has to be real."

"Um, sure," Jonah said.

Katherine tugged on Jonah's arm.

"Here's what happened!" she hissed in his ear. "Wydowse said John Hudson disappeared last—well, I guess it would be last night. He left his dad a note and a map that was supposed to show the Northwest Passage, drawn by this earlier explorer who vanished, named John Cabot. John Hudson supposedly wrote that he was sailing on ahead with some natives in kayaks, and he'd meet his father in the Northwest Passage. . . ."

No wonder Henry Hudson looked so betrayed and confused

when I showed up as John Hudson in the middle of the mutiny, Jonah thought. *No wonder Henry Hudson actually had hope before I appeared, even in the midst of the mutiny—he thought he'd just meet his son and a group of friendly natives a little ways ahead. . . .*

Jonah was trying to puzzle out how things had happened. The real John Hudson would have vanished when Gary and Hodge kidnapped him from time, to take him to be adopted in the future. The real boy wouldn't have had time to leave a note, and wouldn't have known anything about a map. So Second had undoubtedly slipped those onto the ship sometime in the night, to serve his own purposes.

And now he expected Jonah and Katherine to serve his purposes too.

Jonah realized that while Katherine was talking, he'd missed hearing the conversation between Hudson and Staffe and King.

"Huh?" Jonah asked.

"I said, your prayers for deliverance were answered," Staffe replied.

"For now," King said gloomily, staring off into the fog. "We still have no food, we've lost our ship. . . . Shall we sail toward shore, to set up camp at the winter cabin?"

That's what he asked the last time, Jonah thought. *We're back to this whole conversation again. And next, Hudson will say . . .*

"The winter cabin?" Hudson sneered. "Odd's bones, man, we're sailors, not rabbits. At least *I* am. Henry Hudson does not cower in a hole when there are treasure routes to be found, glory to be attained, continents to be conquered."

Jonah's hopes sank. It seemed as if everything important were inevitable; time could only repeat. How could he and Katherine make any changes to save anyone or anything—especially when neither JB nor Second had told them what to do?

Maybe we'll just have to make multiple tries, Jonah thought. *If we come back again and again to the same moment, maybe eventually we'll figure out how to fix it.*

The shallop lurched strangely, practically leaping out of the water. Jonah remembered that the only reason he could relive any of these moments in the shallop was because time was unraveling.

He and Katherine couldn't count on getting multiple chances. He wasn't even sure they had a chance now.

"We've got to do something!" Katherine hissed in his ear. "I don't think we have much time left!"

Jonah turned and glared at his sister.

"Not helping," he whispered back, without moving his lips.

Meanwhile Staffe was trying to persuade Hudson.

"But if we go to the cabin, we can lay in supplies for next winter," Staffe said, taking up John King's argument. "By next spring a rescue expedition is bound to come for us—"

"Henry Hudson will not be *rescued!*" Hudson thundered, smacking his hand down on the side of the shallop just as hard as he had the last time. "Henry Hudson will sail home in glory, with a shipload of treasures from the Orient!"

"You still believe in the Northwest Passage?" one of the sickly, dying sailors murmured. "Even now?"

Jonah realized that the sailor asking that question was Wydowse. Wydowse, who by the end of the day would write the letter Katherine was clutching in her hand, hidden behind Jonah.

Wydowse, who would soon be dead.

"You shall refer to it as the Hudson Passage, henceforth," Hudson said haughtily. "Because I *shall* discover it."

Last time Jonah had heard Hudson say that, he'd still been hoping for JB to rescue him. Jonah had whispered frantically into the Elucidator in his pocket.

Now he knew there was no use trying that.

Everything's up to me and Katherine, Jonah thought. *That's one of the few things JB and Second still agree on.*

The shallop rocked unsteadily, the regular rhythm of the waves turning jerky and unpredictable. Was it possible to actually feel time falling apart? Off in the distance Jonah could see a shadow in the fog—the ship coming back for them from the wrong direction, completely manipulated by Second.

If we get back on that ship, we're locked into that fate, Jonah thought. *Second will be in control all over again, posing as Prickett, leading us to the end of time. And—* Jonah glanced over at Wydowse, who was already reaching into his cloak for his compass. *And Second will murder Wydowse all over again.*

It was odd to focus on the death of one sickly old man when they were faced with worldwide disaster, universal destruction. But the thought of everyone and everything dying was too big for Jonah. It paralyzed him. One man—Jonah could handle saving one man.

It was just like before, when Jonah could only focus on Andrea. Except, of course, that Andrea was beautiful, and Jonah was kind of in love with her.

Wydowse was hideous.

He's going to die no matter what, Jonah thought. *Just look at him.*

Wydowse had hollows in his cheeks, bruises around his mouth, teeth that seemed barely anchored in his gums. But Jonah had just spent an entire day with similarly sickly-looking men who had still somehow managed to raise and lower the sails, scramble up rigging, steer an entire ship through a minefield of ice. Maybe Wydowse wasn't actually as close to death as he looked.

Second kept changing the subject, every time we brought up Wydowse's death, Jonah thought. *It was like . . . like a magician trying to distract the audience: "Look! Look at this empty hat!" While the whole time he's stuffing a handkerchief up his sleeve, keeping it out of sight until the next trick.*

But in Second's case what he was trying to distract them from was a dead body.

Jonah kept staring at Wydowse. Jonah didn't know what JB had ever expected him and Katherine to do to save 1611. He didn't know how they could save Andrea, Brendan, Antonio, and JB from 1600. He didn't know how Second expected them to keep all of time from collapsing.

But he did know a way to keep Wydowse from being murdered. He just had to keep Wydowse and Second apart.

If you only knew how to fix one thing, wasn't that at least a start?

"Maybe . . ." Jonah stopped and cleared his throat. "Maybe Staffe and King are right. Maybe we *should* go to the winter cabin."

Belatedly Jonah remembered that he'd said pretty much the same thing the last time. But that had been only for selfish reasons then, not to help anyone else.

It took the fist slamming into his jaw to remember that Hudson had punched him for saying that before.

Hudson used his other hand to pin Jonah back against the side of the shallop.

"You dare to challenge my authority?" Hudson snarled, looming over Jonah, just as he had before. "I said we will *not* retreat to the winter cabin. We sail on to glory! Do you not remember who is captain here?"

Jonah felt Katherine beside him, practically holding him up.

"You're doing this for Wydowse, aren't you?" she whispered in his ear, and it gave Jonah extra courage, that she was thinking the same way as he was.

Jonah stared into Hudson's eyes. He remembered how he'd felt the last time, how he'd seen so many choices before him. And then all those choices had been taken away from him, because the ship had shown up from the wrong direction, looking so much like their salvation, their rescue. But that wasn't what the ship had been—it wasn't what the ship would be this time around. With Second disguised as Abacuk Prickett at the helm, the ship could only take them toward disaster.

For the first time Jonah thought to wonder what had happened to the real Abacuk Prickett—had Second cast him out on the ice with the mutineers?

Jonah could see Second doing that, and not caring in the least.

Of course, he says he's trying to improve history, Jonah thought. *He's granting Henry Hudson his dearest dream. He's giving the world a true Northwest Passage. He's saving the lives of everyone in this shallop.*

But how did Jonah know that their lives weren't going to be saved anyway? What if John Hudson was supposed to save them?

"Father," Jonah said, still staring directly into Henry Hudson's eyes. "You're not the captain anymore."

He'd considered saying something very much like that before, but he'd known nothing about Hudson then; the words would have come out sounding harsh and mean.

This time he sounded as if he felt sorry for his supposed father, as if he truly regretted insulting him.

Hudson's grip on Jonah's cloak faltered.

"You . . . too?" he murmured. "Even my own son . . . ?"

"I know you want to find the Northwest Passage," Jonah said soothingly. "It's a great dream. But—it's not worth the lives of your own crew. You have to think of your men first. Do you want their blood on your hands?"

Hudson stared at Jonah. Jonah could kind of guess that sea captains in the early 1600s hadn't typically been very concerned about their crews' lives. He realized that what he'd said wasn't really what he wanted to tell Hudson—it was what he wanted to tell Second. Second also had lofty dreams, and he'd gone to great lengths to carry them out: changing 1600, making the *Discovery* sail an impossible route, digging a river that shouldn't exist. But it was all a game to him. Second didn't care about any of the people his changes affected; he acted as if he were only playing with puppets.

Jonah looked up at Staffe and King.

"Do what you know is right," he said. "Set the sails to take us to shore."

They both looked startled but did exactly as he said.

And then Jonah felt the oddest sensation. On almost all his trips through time he had endured a phase where it felt as if every cell in his body—and every atom of every cell—were being pulled apart from every other cell, every other atom. This time Jonah would have sworn that he felt his individual protons, electrons, and neutrons being pulled apart as well. Pulled apart—and then torn again, maybe even ripped in half.

"I feel . . . so strange," Hudson moaned beside him.

The old man slumped over onto the seat—fortunately, he landed just beyond Katherine, because she wouldn't have had time to get out of his way.

"All my dreams, ruined," Hudson mumbled, burying his face in his hands. "Gone, everything's gone."

"Changed," Jonah said gently. "Maybe just postponed?"

But the words sounded distorted to Jonah's ears. He wasn't sure if he'd actually managed to say them aloud.

Jonah realized that everyone else must be feeling the same tearing sensation, too—maybe theirs was even worse than Jonah's. Staffe and King slid down to the floor of the shallop. Wydowse and the other sickly crew members hunched over in agony. Then a new symptom cropped up for Jonah: something like double vision. He could see two versions of everyone in the shallop: two Katherines, both looking see-through and anxious; two Hudsons, one defeated, one defiant; two Staffes, one huddled on the floor, one standing by the mast; two Wydowses, one with his head in his hands, one staring confusedly at a compass.

A compass.

Jonah realized that he was seeing two versions of time at once: the current one, and the way it had gone the last time he and Katherine had been in the shallop. But this wasn't like seeing real time beside tracers with their wispy, ethereal glow. Each version of each person was equally substantial, equally solid. Equally real.

Now Jonah could even see a second version of himself, dressed in John Hudson's cloak, the mask and wig completely disguising his real face and hair. His other self was staring in drop-jawed dismay at . . .

The ship. His other self was watching the *Discovery*, newly returned, hijacked and redirected by Second.

Jonah forgot all caution and grabbed Katherine's arm.

"We can't change anything!" he whispered urgently in her ear. "Any minute now everyone's going to see the ship, and we'll be right back where we started!"

"No!" Katherine whispered back, just as urgently. "I don't think our version of the crew can see that! Look! Isn't John King staring right at it?"

Actually, both John Kings were gazing toward the ship: One was pumping his arm in the air and looking as if he'd just been rescued from almost-certain death. The other one was writhing on the floor in pain, his eyes unfocused and unseeing, even though they were indeed directed toward the ship.

"Think this is another case of time travelers being able to see things others can't?" Jonah asked quietly. "What is this, another time shift, like Second used in 1600?"

"I don't think time shifted," Katherine whispered back. "I think it *split*. See how neither version is fading away?"

This was true. Even as two versions of the shallop and its passengers sailed apart—one toward the *Discovery*, the other toward land—they both stayed substantial and real.

Behind him Jonah heard the sailors in the other shallop calling out, "Huzzah! Huzzah! Hooray!" as they sped toward the *Discovery*.

He heard that shallop's Henry Hudson make his confident boast, "I planned this. I knew it would work out this way."

Nobody currently in the shallop with Jonah seemed to hear any of it. They were still writhing in pain, hunched over in defeat.

"Maybe we're the ones who are going to fade away," Jonah muttered. "Maybe this is how Second planned things. We repair time by—well, with whatever we did—and then we vanish."

"No," Katherine whispered excitedly. "No. We're

going to be okay. Everything's going to work out."

"How can you be so sure?" Jonah asked, shaking his head in disgust.

"Because," Katherine said, and now she was practically squealing. "I see tracers."

THIRTY-FIVE

Katherine was right.

A tracer shallop lay directly ahead of them in the fog, its tracer sails billowing.

"Time's back on track!" Katherine hissed. In her exuberance her voice arced upward, too loudly. The sickly sailor nearest Jonah gazed in her direction with a baffled look on his face.

"Hear that wind?" Jonah said quickly. "Isn't it odd how it sounds almost like a human voice?"

The sailor nodded and slumped back in his seat.

"Shh," Jonah told Katherine, trying to make the sound whistle like wind.

"But this means we succeeded!" Katherine whispered back, keeping her voice pitched only slightly softer. "We did it! If the tracers are back, then original time is back!

We can know what's supposed to happen! We can make everything go the right way!"

Only if we catch up with the tracers, Jonah thought.

"Maybe we should paddle," Jonah said loudly, speaking to the whole boatful now. "We'll get there faster that way."

He dipped his oar in the water. After a moment he saw that John King had inched up from the floor and was paddling as well, opposite Jonah. The shallop sliced through the water, closing in on the tracer version.

With each stroke Jonah felt better. The ripping sensation was gone. Jonah was pretty sure the others in the shallop had gotten over it too. Even the sickliest-looking sailor had straightened up in his seat. Staffe stood by the mast, guiding the sails. Only Henry Hudson still sat with his face buried in his hands.

But—Jonah could see more clearly now—Hudson's tracer was sitting the same way.

The shallop drew near to its tracer version. John King was paddling harder now. The other sailors seemed to be straining forward, drawn toward their tracers.

Jonah remembered that back in 1600, Second had complained about tracers being like fate, trapping people in place. It probably did look that way if you watched the same bits of time again and again, through hundreds of repetitions, as Second had done as a projectionist. But the sailors in this shallop didn't know their fates. They were only straining toward the lives they belonged in.

The shallop lurched into the same space as its tracer. Instantly all the sailors made small adjustments so they matched their tracers exactly. Some scooted slightly to the left; some scooted slightly to the right. Staffe slid his hand a little higher on the mast. Hudson slumped a little lower. King drew his oar back into the boat.

"Right," Jonah said approvingly. "We can give it a rest and just use the sails for now."

King nodded at him, and Jonah wondered what he had been nodding about in original time.

"We didn't build the winter cabin intending it to last past one season," one of the sickly-looking sailors whined.

"It's sturdy enough," Staffe said impatiently. "It'll still be there."

"And we survived *winter* in that cabin," King added. "Won't be nothing to survive there, summertime."

"We can lay up supplies for next winter," Staffe said. "We'll be prepared."

Jonah saw that none of them entirely believed what they were saying. Jonah had once been on a soccer team that lost every game. Before each game the coach always told them lies about how they really were so much better than *these* opponents, and *this* would be the team they finally defeated.

And then Jonah's team would go out on the field and lose 8–0, 10–0, even 12–0 once.

That's what the talk in the shallop reminded Jonah of: his soccer coach's fake pep talks.

And that was only soccer, Jonah thought. *This is life and death.*

He remembered that way back when he and Katherine first arrived in 1611, JB had said, *It's been a hard winter. And spring.* Jonah could read on the faces of every man in the shallop how much they'd already endured.

And what about me and Katherine? Jonah thought. *What can we endure?*

Jonah's excitement at finding the tracers again faded. What good did it do to save time if everyone in the shallop was still doomed?

THIRTY-SIX

Land came into sight. Using the oars again, the sailors maneuvered the shallop into a sort of impromptu dock in the midst of the marshy soil. Across the flat, scrubby land Jonah could see the peak of a roof perhaps a half mile away.

"Cabin still stands," Staffe said, a note of relief in his voice.

"Staffe, you must go ahead and do what you can to make it weathertight again," Hudson said. "King, you shall get the lame sailors to the cabin. I shall supervise getting the shallop to a safe place before that storm arrives."

He nodded his head toward dark clouds on the horizon. Then he looked at Jonah.

What? Jonah wanted to say. Was this the father-son showdown, the battle for control? What would the real John Hudson have done?

Jonah wished he could scoot quickly away from John Hudson's tracer, so he could at least see the expression on his face. But there wasn't time for that.

If I challenge Henry Hudson and say I have to be in control— good grief, what would I tell people to do? Jonah wondered.

"And I, Father?" Jonah said quickly. "What task would you give me?"

Relief flowed over Henry Hudson's face. No second, angrier tracer expression appeared along with the real one, so Jonah guessed that the real John Hudson must have bowed to his father's authority in this moment, too.

For a second Jonah thought Henry Hudson might say, *Thank you, my son. Thank you for giving me my dignity back.* He could feel everyone in the shallop watching the father-son drama.

But then Hudson said only, "You shall go hunt for food."

"Get some scurvy grass, if you can find it," Wydowse murmured.

Jonah had no idea what scurvy grass was, but he was kind of relieved that hunting for food wouldn't involve, well, actual hunting.

Then one of the other sailors half moaned, "Meat."

"Fowl, like we found last winter," another man whispered.

"Deer," another man said.

"Bear," another added.

Okay, they did expect actual hunting. Would it sound too weird if Jonah asked, *What would you have me use as a weapon?* Or did they expect him to kill all those animals with his bare hands?

"Take one of my knives," Staffe said, opening the wooden tool chest he'd brought with him from the ship. He pressed a crude-looking handle into Jonah's palm. The blade attached to it looked rusty and dull, but Jonah supposed it was better than nothing.

"Find a stick to attach it to, and you can use it like a spear," King advised.

Jonah nodded numbly and stepped out of the shallop, because he'd noticed that that was what John Hudson's tracer was doing.

"Now! Finally we're away from all those people!" Katherine exploded beside him as soon as they'd taken a few steps away from the shallop. "Call for JB on the Elucidator!"

Jonah looked at her and blinked. Why hadn't he thought of calling for JB himself?

Because . . . if he could communicate with us right now, wouldn't he already be contacting us? Jonah thought.

Jonah crossed his arms over his chest. He could feel

the Elucidator inside his cloak, pressing against his shirt, poking his skin.

I can't tell Katherine that, Jonah thought. *I should let her keep some hope.*

"Let me concentrate on staying up with John Hudson's tracer," Jonah told her.

Katherine frowned. Jonah half expected her to swing toward the Elucidator and call into it anyway: *JB! JB, hello? Are you there?* But she only squinted at him for a moment and then stepped out of his way, letting him move into the same space as John Hudson's tracer.

Maybe she didn't have much hope right now either.

We'll deal with all of that later, Jonah thought. He'd always been particularly good at procrastinating with things he didn't want to think about. That was part of the reason he'd never asked about his own true identity as a missing child of history.

If Katherine and I die here in 1611, I'll never find out who I really am, Jonah thought.

Somehow that didn't bother him too much. Or maybe it was that he couldn't get past the first part of the sentence: *If Katherine and I die here in 1611 . . .*

Staying alongside John Hudson's tracer, Jonah and Katherine moved farther and farther away from the shallop, away from the men, who were beginning a slow, unsteady trek toward the cabin. It would be completely safe now for Jonah and Katherine to talk out loud, to figure out exactly what had happened out on the water, to debate their options going forward. But Katherine stayed silent, and so Jonah did too.

Maybe it's too scary to talk about what everything means, and what we think is going to happen next? Jonah thought.

He'd felt so odd in that moment when everything doubled and split. His mind shied away from thinking about it, just as his mind had shied away from similar oddities that Second had orchestrated in 1600. It was easiest just to concentrate on walking forward, moving and looking around at the same pace as John Hudson's tracer.

The ground beneath his feet became less marshy. The tracer's jaw dropped suddenly, and he took off running toward a stand of short plants with small white flowers and spoon-shaped leaves. He began hacking at the plants with the dull knife.

"You think that's scurvy grass?" Katherine asked.

The tracer stuck a leaf of it in his mouth, so Jonah and Katherine did the same. Katherine quickly spat hers out.

"I don't think they're asking for it because of the taste," she muttered.

Jonah tried to cut as much of it as the tracer did. The

tracer tucked the scurvy grass in the hood of his cloak, so Jonah did the same.

As they moved on, Jonah expected the tracer to find a stick to use to make a spear, as John King had suggested back in the shallop. After a few moments Jonah realized that that was one of the things that the tracer was looking for, as he peered around. But there weren't any sticks lying around on the ground. And the nearest trees were miles away, just clumps on the horizon, as dark and foreboding as the clouds.

"What did you say the native people in this area are called?" Jonah asked Katherine, because that, at least, was a safe thing to talk about.

"Um—Inuits?" Katherine answered.

"*They* survive in this environment, so it's possible, right?" Jonah asked.

"Do you see any of them around here, rushing out to greet their new neighbors?" Katherine asked. "Do you see any sign that anyone lives here?"

Okay, maybe that wasn't such a safe topic. Maybe it was possible for people to live down in the area by the fake river Second had created, or would create, or however Jonah was supposed to think of that other time. That didn't mean that it was possible for people to survive here for very long.

Especially if they were a bunch of English sailors, without food or other supplies, who weren't familiar with the area.

And what about two kids from the twenty-first century? Jonah wondered.

And then he didn't have time to think about such unpleasant topics, because the tracer John Hudson froze, a look of panic on his face.

"What's his problem?" Katherine whispered. She turned to gaze in the same direction as the tracer. "Oh. Oh, no. . . ."

Jonah looked too. At first he thought that the land around them wasn't as flat as he'd first thought. There was a small, dark hill right in front of them.

Then the "hill" moved.

It wasn't a hill.

It was a bear.

THIRTY-SEVEN

"Run!" Katherine shrieked.

"Er—is a bear one of those animals you should run away from? Or one where you should freeze and not show fear?" Jonah asked. He forgot he was supposed to be hunting. His mind blanked. His knees locked. He might have to freeze just because he couldn't get his body to do anything else.

"But it's running toward us!" Katherine screamed.

She grabbed Jonah's arm and pulled him along, and Jonah discovered he was capable of running after all. John Hudson's tracer turned and ran as well, and Jonah felt closer to John Hudson than ever. John Hudson had to be thinking exactly what Jonah was: *I'm going to die, I'm going to die, I'm going to die . . .*

The bear growled then, a sound that seemed to shake

the earth. Or maybe it was the bear's paws hitting the ground that caused tremors.

Jonah's vision went splotchy. He was running so hard that his head was jarring up and down; his gaze was bobbing all over the place. But he could see a dark blob ahead of them.

"That's a cub!" Jonah screamed. "You—never—get—between—a—bear—and—its—cub!"

Jonah, Katherine, and John Hudson's tracer all veered away from the cub at the same time. But the tracer was thinking one step ahead of Jonah: He had his rusty knife low in his hand, the blade ready.

"Knife!" Katherine screamed at Jonah. "Get out your knife!"

It's got a three-inch handle! Jonah wanted to scream back at her. *I couldn't survive getting three inches away from those claws!*

There wasn't enough air in his lungs to say anything. But Jonah imitated the way the tracer was holding the knife.

Guess I've still got some hope left, Jonah thought.

He gulped in a quick breath and dared to throw a glance over his shoulder. The bear was even closer than Jonah thought. It reared up on its hind legs and roared again.

"You go that way!" Jonah yelled at Katherine. He pointed away from the cub. "I—I'll stay and fight!"

"We fight together!" Katherine yelled back at him.

"We've only got one knife!"

Screaming at Katherine gave him enough courage to act. He shoved Katherine out of the way and slashed the knife blindly at the bear. Without thinking about it, he mimicked the tracer's motion. Jonah's knife and the tracer's knife cut into the exact same spot on the bear's gut.

And both knives stuck there, swallowed up in the fur.

The bear roared louder and slashed a front paw toward Jonah. Jonah didn't have time to react. The paw came closer and closer and closer . . .

And then the bear whirled to the side, because Katherine was kicking its left leg.

"Divide and conquer!" Katherine screamed. "You hit the other side!"

Jonah saw something falling toward him, but it was only the tracer bear, attacking the tracer John Hudson. Jonah didn't have time to worry about the fate of tracers when his real sister was in danger. Jonah took a step closer to the bear and reached for the knife.

I can twist it, Jonah thought. *Twist the knife, distract the bear, save Katherine . . .*

Jonah couldn't find the knife. He settled for punching the bear's gut.

Oh—there's the knife!

His punch landed directly on the handle, driving the blade deeper into the bear's fur. The bear howled and swiped both front paws toward Jonah.

No hope now, Jonah thought. *No hope, no hope.*

Everything went black.

THIRTY-EIGHT

Jonah woke up.

This surprised him. His mind still held the image of the two huge bear paws swinging toward him—people didn't wake up after being hit by something like that. Or, if they did, they were in excruciating pain, gushing blood, on the verge of death.

Jonah felt fine. Just a little groggy. And he couldn't see anything, but that might have been because he was lying in the dark.

"Is this heaven?" a voice whispered beside him. Katherine's voice.

Someone laughed.

"You two didn't *die*. You think I'd let that happen to you? After everything you've done for me? With everything you've still got left to do in the future?"

Jonah couldn't quite identify the voice. It was too distorted, too far away. Or maybe it was close by and normal, but Jonah wasn't hearing it right. In fact, his ears seemed as messed up as they always did when he had . . .

Timesickness.

"Out of time," he murmured. "You pulled us out." Jonah had trouble pronouncing the words, which confirmed it. "But . . . where are we now?"

"Some kind of time hollow, I think," Katherine whispered beside him. Once again she seemed to be recovering faster than Jonah.

"It would be delightful to just watch the two of you figure everything out, but time is of the essence," the voice said. "We need to move this along."

"That's Second talking," Jonah said. Disappointment seeped through him—he'd wanted it to be JB. He'd wanted JB to be there, assuring them that they'd done everything right, everything was over, everyone was safe.

"But Second's not here, is he?" Katherine asked. Jonah could see just well enough to tell that she was peering around and reaching out into the darkness. "He's just talking to us through . . ."

"The Elucidator," Jonah said.

He pulled the Elucidator out of his cloak, and it instantly began to glow, showing that it had transformed from its 1600s candleholder shape to something more like a cell phone.

"You deserve a reward for your deductions," Second's voice came out of the Elucidator. "So—let there be light."

The Elucidator grew brighter, illuminating an empty, windowless, sterile, safe room.

No bear was charging at them. No danger lay in this space at all.

It didn't matter. Jonah kept seeing the bear's paws swiping toward him. He kept feeling echoes of the terror he'd felt just a moment ago—his heart pounded as if his brain were still screaming at him, *I'm going to die, I'm going to die, I'm going to die . . .*

Jonah began shaking the Elucidator.

"Why'd you let that go on so long?" he demanded. "Why didn't you pull us out sooner? You could have done it as soon as I was out of sight of all the men from the shallop. Or even before that—when time split, or whatever that was. Katherine and I could have died!"

"Calm down—stop that! You'll break the Elucidator!" Second cried. "I had to wait until you punched the knife—the knife had to go in as deep as the tracer's knife, so the bear would bleed enough that Hudson's men could follow the trail of blood. When they saw the knife, they figured out that the bear had killed John Hudson. And the bear was weak enough from its wound that they could kill it. The meat kept them alive and gave them something to trade with the natives, when they met them. . . ."

Second said all that in an offhand way, as if the bear dying and John Hudson dying and the other men living were all just facts from the past, requirements of time—no more interesting or important than *i*'s that had to be dotted and *t*'s that had to be crossed. And now it was over and done, and that was all Second cared about.

But Jonah had felt the bear's hot breath on his face. He'd felt awe along with his terror, seeing the massive bear rear up on its hind legs.

My puny knife helped kill that? he marveled.

And Jonah had spent practically an entire day living John Hudson's life. He'd taken the scorn aimed at John Hudson: the one mutineer bragging about giving the "pup" what he deserved; the other mutineer jibing that the shallop needed a ship's boy; John King slamming the top of the stocks down on Jonah's neck.

And Jonah had gotten the care and concern John Hudson had earned. He'd heard Staffe tell him, *The wrong Hudson is captain of this ship.* He'd seen practically the entire shipload of sailors avert their eyes when Jonah was trapped in the stocks.

And Jonah had been in the shallop with everyone else,

just as much in fear for his life as any of them.

"Who died?" Jonah asked. "Who lived? Who did I save, punching that knife?"

"Well, they all died eventually," Second said. "That's how it works. People live, they die, time goes on. . . ."

"You know what he means!" Katherine interrupted.

"Philip Staffe survived," Second said. "He married a native woman, had children . . . as far as I could tell by watching, he had a happy life."

I helped save Staffe's life, Jonah thought. *My few moments of terror—okay, they were worth it for Staffe's life.*

"And the others?" Katherine asked.

"Not such happy endings," Second said. "Hudson pretty much went mad with grief when his son died. John King died of a mysterious fever. Wydowse only lived another month."

"That's a month more than you would have given him!" Jonah protested.

"As I was saying before," Second said in a steely voice. "We really do need to move this along."

"Why?" Katherine asked. "We're in a safe place. Time doesn't move in a time hollow. We could ask you questions all day."

"No," Second said. "Not this time. Not in this hollow."

Jonah felt a shiver of foreboding crawl down his spine.

"What are you talking about?" he asked.

"We're almost out of time," Second said. "Because in a few minutes JB's going to show up."

"He's safe?" Jonah cried. "Then—so are Brendan and Antonio and—and Andrea! Andrea! You're keeping your deal! You're letting them out of 1600!"

"It's not time to call in the deal yet," Second said, in such a solemn voice that Jonah stopped exulting instantly. "This isn't going to be JB after he's rescued from 1600. This is JB before. On his way into danger to rescue you."

THIRTY-NINE

Jonah's brain short-circuited. It wasn't enough that he'd had to deal with a bear, a mutiny, ice floes, a clubbing, and life-and-death impersonation. Now he was supposed to figure out Second's scrambled sense of time, too?

"JB's coming from before his trip to 1600, but we're after it," Katherine said slowly. "So . . ."

"So technically this type of interaction is completely prohibited, because the time police are always convinced that time travelers meeting from opposites sides of a visit would cause serious paradoxes," Second said. "But they think *everything* could cause paradoxes, and this is actually going to finish healing time. All you have to do is tell him to go to Croatoan Island on August 3, 1600. And hand him the Elucidator. Don't tell him anything else."

"No," Jonah said.

Katherine looked at her brother.

"I'm with Jonah," she said. "No."

"No, what?" Second said, and now his voice carried a note of frustration. "No, you won't give him the Elucidator? No, you won't tell him to go to Croatoan Island?"

"Oh, we'll do that," Jonah said. "But we'll tell him other stuff too."

"Everything," Katherine said.

Jonah grinned at her, and nodded.

"What?" Second cried. "Don't you understand the danger of paradoxes?"

"We understand that you have been using us," Jonah said. His voice grew more confident with each word. "We understand that we're just puppets to you. Just like Hudson's men were puppets to him, until they rose up and told him different."

"And we're not going to do that to JB," Katherine said, finishing for Jonah. "We're not going to send him into the dangers of 1600 without warning him first."

"But—but—this is preposterous!" Second sputtered. "You're children! You don't know what you're doing! You could make time collapse after all! This—this voids our deal!"

"All you said was that we had to help you in 1611!"

Jonah said. "You didn't say we had to be your slaves forever! You didn't say we had to obey your every command! You—"

And then Jonah stopped talking, because the air before them was shimmering. A moment later, JB appeared.

Jonah had seen JB in numerous stressful situations in the past—*er, would it be in the future?*—but JB had always exuded a certain confidence and certainty. Part of it was that he was really good-looking. Even before they knew who he was, Katherine had taken one look at·JB's dark hair and dark eyes and handsome features and begun calling him "cute janitor boy."

JB didn't look so handsome now. Or confident or certain. He had dark circles under his eyes; his mouth was drawn into an anxious frown; his hair was so messed up that it looked as if it'd been days since he'd washed or combed it.

Had he looked this bad when they saw him arriving in 1600? Or had Jonah and Katherine been too stressed out to notice?

"JB?" Katherine said hesitantly, as if she didn't quite recognize him in such an unkempt state.

JB squinted at her. Jonah had gotten so used to Katherine being nearly invisible that he'd stopped thinking about it. But JB acted as if he couldn't trust anyone who looked so much like crystal.

"Katherine?" JB asked. "Is that really you? Or just another one of Second's tricks? I've followed so many of his blind alleys, but this time, coming to this time hollow, I thought—I hoped that—"

"Of course it's us!" Jonah said.

JB's squint deepened as he turned to Jonah.

"Who are you?" JB asked.

Jonah had forgotten that he was still disguised as John Hudson—probably looking worse than ever after his day in the stocks, his repeated time in the shallop, and his encounter with the bear.

Jonah tugged at his mask, but he couldn't get it to budge.

"I'm Jonah!" he protested, but of course his voice came out sounding all wrong. In the past day Jonah had almost stopped noticing how different his John Hudson voice was from his usual voice, but now the weirdness came back to him.

He wasn't surprised that JB backed away from him.

"Nice try, Second," JB muttered. "But unless these holograms—are they holograms?—unless one of you can tell me where to find the real Jonah and Katherine and Andrea, I'm out of here."

"We—," Katherine began.

Quickly Jonah clapped his hand over his sister's mouth.

"Don't tell yet!" he commanded.

Katherine blinked at him.

"I was just going to say that we *are* the real Jonah and Katherine," she muttered, her words muffled by Jonah's hand.

"I'm in a hurry, kids," JB said. "I don't have time for this."

"Yes, you do," Jonah said. He tried to think of something he could tell JB that would make it clear who they were. But before he went rogue, Second had been JB's trusted projectionist; if he had created holograms or some other fake version of Jonah and Katherine, he could give them any secret knowledge he wanted.

This was awful. Jonah was going to have to resort to the same kind of tactics Second used.

"You have to listen to us," Jonah said. "Because we have information you need. And we're not going to give it to you until you listen to our whole story."

FORTY

It felt as if it took hours to tell everything, even in the time hollow, where time didn't move. Maybe things would have gone better if Jonah had let Katherine tell the whole story by herself, or if Katherine had let Jonah tell it all. But neither of them could resist constantly interrupting—"No, the book I found on Hudson's ship with Andrea's picture in it wasn't *New Visions of the New World;* it was *New Views of the New World.*" "You know, I was freezing the whole time I was in 1611. If this is pretty much a do-over, is there any way you could get me a coat this time around?" "I *had* to crash into Henry Hudson's room when I thought the sailors had found Katherine! What else could I have done?" "Wait—isn't this kind of like proof? Look at these papers that I took from Wydowse's desk!"

Jonah expected Second to chip in too, with his version

of events. Or perhaps with the information that JB truly wanted.

But the Elucidator stayed silent.

Finally Jonah and Katherine were done.

"So, do you believe us?" Katherine asked.

JB frowned.

"I don't *want* to," he said. "But . . ." He leafed through Wydowse's papers for the third or fourth time, as if he hoped the words on them would change. He sighed. "Let me see that Elucidator."

Jonah handed it over. JB pressed a few buttons, then held it up to his ear. Then he lifted his own Elucidator to his mouth.

"We didn't know what we were doing," he said in a tense voice, into the Elucidator. He hit something on the Elucidator, then spoke again. "Jonah? Katherine? We tried. We really tried. . . ." Another pause. More button-pushing. "Who else would it be?" Pause again. "*Second* was talking to you again? Oh, no. . . ."

Katherine gasped.

"That's all the stuff you said to us when we first got to 1611!" she exclaimed. "What are you doing? Are you *recording* that?"

JB lowered the Elucidator and peered over at her and Jonah.

"If everything you just told me is true, I'm not really going to be able to talk to you from 1600," JB said.

"What?" Jonah asked. "Then—that's all fake, too? Another setup? None of it's true?"

JB looked at the screen of the Elucidator Jonah had been carrying.

"Oh, by the time you hear it in 1611, it will be true all right," JB said. "Just not the whole truth." He read something from the screen. "'I see that we made even more mistakes than I thought'—oh, yes, absolutely. Truer words have never been spoken."

"But—when we're in 1611, we're going to *believe* that you're talking to us from 1600," Katherine protested. "We're going to believe that you're all right."

"And that Andrea's all right," Jonah added. "And Brendan and Antonio."

"Well, none of us can survive unless you believe that we *have*," JB said. "Everything collapses unless you have faith enough to keep going, to get here, so you can tell me how to save you in 1600, and begin the cycle all over again." He flashed them a pained grin. "It's kind of a conundrum, isn't it?"

Jonah's head ached trying to straighten it all out. He watched in silence as JB finished recording the comments that Jonah had already heard him make. Then JB pressed the two Elucidators together.

"This will transfer the alarm and siren sound effects," JB muttered. "And all of Second's recorded comments."

"You're doing that on purpose? You're letting Second have all the control?" Jonah asked incredulously.

"I am working within the trap that Second set for us all," JB said. "When you're in a cage and someone hands you a key, you take it."

He stood up and handed Jonah one of the Elucidators.

"Don't go," Katherine said. "Or—take us with you. Or—"

It didn't seem as if she could settle on the right solution.

JB grimaced.

"We all know what I have to do now," he said. "I just hope there aren't any hidden traps I don't know about." He hesitated. "Are you sure when you were traveling from 1600 to 1611, you were leapfrogging back and forth with the ripple of changes Second unleashed?"

"That's not something we could forget," Jonah said sarcastically. Crossing the ripple again and again had been like riding an amusement-park ride designed by a madman.

"But we got to 1611 before the ripple," Katherine added. "We landed, and then the book with the picture of Andrea fell on Jonah's face."

JB nodded grimly.

"Then Second calibrated all of this very, very closely. We have to play it his way," he said.

He began typing coordinates into his Elucidator. Katherine took a step toward him, and for a minute Jonah was afraid that she was going to grab JB and refuse to let go.

Instead she pulled a lock of his hair down onto his forehead.

"What?" she said, when Jonah—and JB—stared at her in confusion. "That was something I noticed when you arrived in 1600—the way your hair looked."

Jonah and JB both rolled their eyes.

"But what should we do now?" Jonah asked, and he was ashamed that his voice cracked.

"Do a search for 'costume removal' on your Elucidator," JB said. "I've programmed it to be easy for you to use. Follow the directions exactly. And then . . . then, if I don't come back, type in your home phone number and hit enter. That should take you somewhere safe."

"Should?" Katherine echoed forlornly.

"When we've opened up even the past for revision, what certainty can anyone offer about the future?" JB asked.

"But—," Jonah began.

JB was already gone.

FORTY-ONE

Like a fool Jonah dashed to the spot where JB had been standing. Jonah even swiped his hands at the empty air a few times before he could convince himself it was useless. He expected Katherine to laugh at him—until he realized Katherine was doing the same thing.

"Ahem," Jonah said, clearing his throat and dropping his hands to his side. "Just . . . getting a little exercise . . ."

"Right," Katherine said, shaking her head.

She lowered her hands as well.

And then they both stood there, helpless.

"Um, costume removal?" Katherine said.

"Sure," Jonah agreed.

He didn't want to look and sound like John Hudson a second longer. But he found himself moving slowly as he lifted the Elucidator to look at the screen.

What if we finish with that really quickly and then we have nothing to distract us and JB still isn't back? How long would we wait before we'd give up? Jonah wondered.

Fortunately, getting rid of the John Hudson costume appeared to be a complicated process. First, they had to figure out how to do a search on the Elucidator—the problem was that it was about a million times more advanced than an iPhone. You barely had to think about typing or swiping at the screen and the Elucidator was already obeying. But that meant that Jonah and Katherine kept giving it conflicting commands.

"Here it is—how to remove a historical costume you no longer need," Katherine finally said. "You just . . ."

"Wait—if I get rid of the costume, what will that leave me to wear?" Jonah asked. "Do I get my old clothes back, or what?"

Katherine wrinkled up her nose. "Oh, right, let's make sure you're not going to be sitting here in your underwear," she muttered.

Jonah decided not to tell her that his 1611 costume didn't include underwear.

The two of them had to read tons of fine print, but eventually they found the proper commands to type in. Instantly Jonah was back in the T-shirt and jeans he'd worn first to 1600, and then to 1611. The T-shirt still had sweat stains from his time on Roanoke and Croatoan islands; the jeans were stiff with a crust of sand from the knees on down.

· "Do I look normal now?" Jonah asked his sister.

"What do you mean? You've never looked normal," she answered.

But her eyes shone.

It was only a second later that both of them began looking around, waiting for JB to reappear. The costume change had been a good distraction, but it hadn't lasted long enough.

"Second, can't you tell us if JB is coming back?" Jonah asked the Elucidator.

The Elucidator was silent.

"Jonah, I don't think he was ever really talking to us here," Katherine said. "I think everything he said over the Elucidator was prerecorded, too."

"But—he answered our other questions! How did he know what we were going to ask?" Jonah asked.

"Voice-activated prompts," Katherine said. "Like on a phone. 'For store hours, press or say, one. For store directions, press or say, two,'" she imitated in a robotic voice.

"For assurance that you didn't die, mention the word 'heaven,'" Jonah said bitterly. "And if you ask anything I don't really want to answer, I'll just tell you, 'We need to move this along.' Ergh! You're right! Remember, he did the same kind of thing before? When we were traveling to 1611?"

He shook the Elucidator in frustration. Katherine must have thought he was actually so upset he might throw it, because she grabbed his arm.

"Jonah! That could be our only way out of here!" she complained, jerking on his elbow.

"No, no, I'm certain JB will be back in an instant, and we can get out of here with *his* Elucidator," Jonah said sarcastically.

Katherine stopped pulling on Jonah's arm. She let go completely.

"Oh, no. Oh, no," she said, practically hyperventilating.

"What's wrong?" Jonah asked.

"*That's* why JB hasn't come back yet," Katherine said.

"Huh?"

Katherine leaned forward, her hands on her knees. She seemed to be trying to catch her breath. She turned her head to look at Jonah.

"Because we have his Elucidator," she said. "Remember? He gave it to us when we left 1600."

FORTY-TWO

Just once Jonah wanted to figure out something about time before Katherine did.

Or, right now, he'd settle for proving her wrong.

"No! That can't be right!" he protested. "It's—JB was talking to us on this Elucidator when we were traveling from 1600 to 1611. That has to mean he had a second Elucidator with him!"

"That could have been another prerecorded message," Katherine argued. "Second could have even created it, faking JB's voice."

Jonah couldn't deny it. If Jonah could sound like John Hudson, Second could undoubtedly make an Elucidator sound like JB.

"But we told JB everything we heard him say, and he didn't object to any of it, so those weren't *lies*," Jonah began, trying to puzzle everything out. Then he realized that that wasn't the important issue right now. "Anyhow, Andrea had an Elucidator with her too. They could all use that one to escape. Remember? The one she got from Second?"

"You'd trust an Elucidator that came from Second?" Katherine asked, making a face. "He probably set it to malfunction too. If any of them had a working Elucidator, don't you think JB would be back by now?"

She had a point. But he could kind of see where she was going with this, and he didn't like it.

Then he thought of something he liked even less.

I've changed my mind, he thought. *I don't want to figure out anything about time ahead of Katherine. I don't want to figure out anything. I just want to hide out here in this time hollow, bury my head in the sand . . .*

"What's wrong?" Katherine said. "You look really pale. Did you hit the 'turn invisible' button on the Elucidator?"

"I'm thinking," Jonah said.

"Well, there's a first time for everything," Katherine said. But Jonah could tell that her heart wasn't in the insult. She didn't add to it, the way she normally would. She just fell silent, and waited.

"We both think this Elucidator is the same one JB had

in here a few minutes ago, right?" Jonah asked, holding up the Elucidator.

Katherine nodded.

"Sure," she said. "We just saw him load it up with all the things he said to us when we got to 1611. Of course it's the same."

"Then . . . this one object was here twice—in my hand and in JB's," Jonah said slowly. "We know that, under the usual rules of time, there can't be two versions of the same person in the same time. So wouldn't that same rule apply to objects?"

"Oh, but the rules can change," Katherine said. "When . . ."

"Time's unraveling," Jonah finished.

Katherine's eyes got big.

"Then we didn't fix everything, when we went back to the shallop," she said. "Time's still falling apart."

"Maybe my theory's wrong," Jonah admitted. "Maybe there are rules we don't know about, for normal time. Maybe all bets are off in a time hollow. Maybe objects can duplicate all they want."

Katherine was shaking her head.

"No, you've got to be right about all this," she said. She put her hands up to her face. "You know what this means, don't you?"

Jonah bit his lip.

"Everything still depends on us," he said. "If there's even a chance that we're the only ones with an Elucidator, we've got to help. We've got to go rescue JB and the others."

FORTY-THREE

Jonah was a "rip Band-Aids off as quick as possible" kind of kid. If he had to do anything that required even the slightest hint of bravery, he wanted to do it immediately, before he had time to think.

So what they did next practically killed him:

Research.

"Come on! Let's just go!" he begged Katherine.

"Go *where?*" she asked him, looking up from the Elucidator she'd grabbed from Jonah's hand. "For once let's do this intelligently. Let's make some plans." She seemed to be scrolling through screen after screen after screen of information. She sighed. "I'm getting sick of typing. Can we try voice commands?" she asked it. "Where's JB right now?"

A single word glowed on the screen: **WHEN?** Then

that was replaced with WHICH 'RIGHT NOW' ARE YOU TALKING ABOUT?

Katherine sighed again.

"Oh, right," she said. "I should have remembered."

They weren't in time, so there was no such thing as "right now."

"Let's just follow JB back to 1600," Jonah said. "Like, a minute or two after he sent us away?"

THAT'S DAMAGED TIME, the Elucidator flashed at him. NO TIME TRAVELERS ALLOWED IN OR OUT.

"Wait a minute," Katherine said. "Brendan and Antonio and Andrea got back into that time."

WHAT DO YOU THINK DAMAGED IT? the Elucidator asked.

Jonah shivered.

"Then take us to JB in the first moment we're allowed in!" he insisted.

OK, flashed on the computer screen.

Jonah immediately began feeling dizzy.

"Jonah! It's obeying you!" Katherine shrieked. "Wait! Stop! We haven't planned anything yet! We don't know where we're going! We—"

The screen flashed: TOO LATE. CAN'T STOP.

And then Jonah and Katherine were zipping back through time.

FORTY-FOUR

"Don't you ever pay attention to any of those guidance assemblies at school?" Katherine demanded as they floated through the darkness of Outer Time.

"Huh?" Jonah said.

"You know, when they talk about impulse control, about how you shouldn't just do or say anything you feel like, anytime you feel like doing or saying it?" Katherine said. "How that's what growing up is all about?"

"Honestly?" Jonah said. "No."

He wished Katherine would shut up, so maybe they could ask the Elucidator where they were going, and what they would face when they arrived. Maybe they could tell the Elucidator to make him invisible too.

But how could he suggest that without admitting that they should have done all that already?

He was still debating this when suddenly everything

sped up. Lights zoomed at them. Jonah felt as if his body were being torn apart; gravity and time and all the other forces of the universe seemed to be tugging him in opposite directions.

And then everything stopped. They'd landed.

"Hot," Katherine moaned. "Too hot."

Probably . . . new symptom of timesickness, Jonah thought irritably. He was more annoyed than ever with the creaky way his timesick brain worked. *Come on. . . . Come on. . . . Function!*

He tried to stretch his fingers out, feeling for the Elucidator, but his fingers weren't working any better than his brain.

Oh, right. Katherine was holding the Elucidator, not me. And I know Katherine's timesick too, because she said she was hot. . . .

Dimly Jonah remembered that they'd been cold landing on Hudson's ship, and that that hadn't been a timesickness symptom. It really had been cold and icy.

So maybe the heat was real too?

Duh. The last we knew of JB, it was August 1600, and he was in what's going to be North Carolina. It'd make sense that we're hot, if this is still North Carolina in August. Or August again.

Jonah's brain got hung up for a ridiculously long time on the notion that this could be a different August from 1600, and they could still be near JB. JB and Andrea and Brendan and Antonio might have lived through all of

1600 and all of 1601 and all of 1602 and . . .

Does it really get this *hot in North Carolina in the summertime?* Jonah wondered. *This feels more like, I don't know . . . fire?*

Jonah's faulty brain spun a bit of poetry at him that his seventh-grade English teacher liked to quote whenever the heat or air conditioning in her classroom malfunctioned, as it often did: *"Some say the world will end in fire, / Some say in ice . . ."*

She'd always laughed about it, but Jonah didn't see the world ending as a joking matter anymore.

It felt like the world could have ended in ice on Hudson's ship, Jonah thought. *And now, and now . . .*

He realized that he'd been keeping his eyes closed, because his eyelids felt so hot and baked and uncomfortable. Like he really was lying right beside a crackling fire. Maybe he should open them and see if that might be true? And then maybe try to roll away?

He got his swollen eyelids open a crack. He did indeed seem to be staring into flames. He opened his eyes a little wider.

He saw more flames.

He opened his eyes all the way, and still he could see nothing but fire. He was staring into a huge wall of flames.

Advancing right toward him and Katherine.

FORTY-FIVE

"Fire!" Jonah screamed. "Fire!"

"Shh," Katherine whispered beside him. "Not supposed . . . to disturb time. Not change . . ."

The firelight glowed through her—she was still mostly invisible.

"Can you run?" Jonah shouted at her.

"Run?" she murmured. "Can't . . . even . . . move . . . yet."

Jonah grabbed the Elucidator from her hand.

"Send Katherine back to the time hollow!" he yelled into it.

Katherine vanished.

Jonah sat there panting for a moment, trying to draw oxygen from the baked air into his lungs.

Impulse control, he thought. *Right. Duh. Why didn't I think before I started yelling at the Elucidator? Why didn't I send myself back with Katherine?*

It seemed as if there had been some reason he hadn't wanted to, some reason he shouldn't ask to be zapped directly back to safety right now.

He'd just forgotten what it was.

He looked around, trying to focus his eyes on something besides the flames lapping toward him. Dark black lines stood out in the flames—*trees*, Jonah realized. *That's a forest fire I'm watching.*

What was he doing in a forest fire? They'd been on a beach the last time he'd seen . . .

JB, Jonah remembered. *I can't leave until I rescue JB.*

He turned his head the other way and saw JB lying on the ground. It was a struggle, but Jonah managed to half crawl, half stumble toward JB. He grabbed the man's shoulders and shook them hard.

"JB! Wake up!" he shouted. "We've got to get out of here! Where's everyone else? Brendan and Antonio and . . . and Andrea . . ."

JB didn't move. He seemed to be struggling to breathe.

Is this what happens when someone passes out from smoke inhalation? Jonah wondered.

His brain wasn't working well enough to figure it out. Except—shouldn't JB get out of the smoke?

"Send JB back with Katherine!" Jonah yelled into the Elucidator.

JB vanished too.

Something crashed down from above, landing in the exact spot where JB's face had been only a moment earlier. Whatever it was, it was on fire.

Roof, Jonah thought. *Roof falling in.*

He realized that he was in a hut—or the remains of a hut. One side of it had already been eaten away by flames.

Jonah had to get out. But—

"JB, were you alone in here?" he shouted.

He started groping around on the ground, wincing because he kept touching sparks. Then he noticed a new message glowing on the Elucidator screen: **HE WAS ALONE.**

"Great! Now you tell me!" Jonah mumbled, staggering out the door.

He found himself in the center of a cluster of huts—a familiar-looking place, because he'd seen Native American villages like this on his last trip to 1600. Only he hadn't seen any of those villages bursting into flame.

"Where are Andrea and Brendan and Antonio?" he yelled at the Elucidator.

IN OTHER HUTS, shone on the Elucidator screen.

"Thanks a lot!" he yelled. "Can't you be more specific?"

Then he got distracted, because a man ran past him carrying a huge carved figure.

"Hey!" Jonah yelled at him. "Why don't you save the people before the artwork?"

For just an instant the man and the carving were silhouetted against the flames.

Then they both vanished.

Artwork, Jonah thought. *Brendan and Antonio are artists . . .*

He remembered what JB had told his friends Brendan and Antonio about their lives in original time in the early 1600s. A fire had swept through their village, killing them and destroying all their art. But when time travelers discovered the brilliance of their work, some people from the future had illegally come back to steal the art right before it burned.

The running man had to be one of those time travelers.

So this must be the fire that's going to kill them.

"No! I won't let it!" Jonah screamed.

He ran to the door of the next hut.

"Brendan? Antonio? Andrea?" he called.

Small children stirred on the floor of the hut and looked up at him drowsily. Their eyes widened when they saw the glow of the flames behind him.

"Run!" they cried out. "Mama! Papa! Wake up! We have to run!"

The fear in their voices was so strong that Jonah thought he would have understood even without any translation help.

"Yeah—run!" he said. "Great idea!"

He looked back at the flames, which were even closer now. They stretched from horizon to horizon, eating up everything in their path.

Small children couldn't outrun that. Nobody could.

Jonah made a snap decision.

"Send everyone from this hut into the time hollow with JB and Katherine!" he yelled at the Elucidator.

Instantly the hut was empty.

He ran to the next hut and yelled the same thing. And the next one. And the next one. And the next one.

Jonah didn't count the huts he ran to. He didn't count the people he saved. He didn't even really look at any of them. He just zigzagged back and forth, hut to hut to hut, yelling the same phrase into the Elucidator again and again and again. By the second-to-last hut, he could barely squeeze out the words from his dry, scratchy throat. He could barely see through the smoke. Flames licked at his heels.

One more, he told himself, forcing himself onward. *Just one more.*

He fell to his hands and knees. His elbows collapsed under him, and then he could do nothing but squirm forward through the dirt.

But it's better down here, he told himself. *Less smoke.*

He rolled over, just enough to get his head into the last hut. He squinted. Was anybody in here? Was that an old man cowering in the corner? Was a boy patting the old man's arm?

They might have been figments of Jonah's imagination, illusions formed in the smoke. But he croaked out anyway, "Send everyone from this hut back to the time hollow."

He paused. Was he forgetting something? He just wanted to sleep—to shut his eyes against the smoke that stung them, close his mouth and nose to the burning air, drop into some oblivion where the flames climbing the walls wouldn't matter. But Katherine always got so mad at him for forgetting things, for failing to think ahead. Was there something else he needed to do before he slept?

"Oh . . . yeah," he said painfully, each word causing a new ache. "Send . . . me . . . too."

FORTY-SIX

Jonah woke to cheering.

"It's the boy who saved us!"

"He lives too!"

"Jonah!"

Then he heard Katherine say sarcastically, "And I thought you looked bad in the John Hudson costume. Have you been rolling in mud—or ashes?"

She threw her arms around his shoulders. Someone had turned her completely visible once again, but for a minute Jonah couldn't tell if she was going to hug him or beat him up.

"You idiot! I thought you were dead! All these other people kept showing up, but not you." She choked on a half sob. "Why didn't you let me stay and help?"

"You were practically comatose!" Jonah protested.

"I wouldn't have been, if you'd given me an extra minute to recover from the timesickness," Katherine said.

"We didn't *have* an extra minute," Jonah said.

Katherine's grip on his shoulders turned into a real hug. She seemed to have forgotten about the mud and the ash.

"You really scared me," she whispered.

"Can I talk to him?" another voice said softly behind Katherine.

It was Andrea.

Katherine pulled back, letting Jonah see past her. At least he *should* have been able to. He sat up and blinked hard, trying to get his eyes to work right. Now he could see a crowd of dark-haired people—all the Native Americans from the village. And he could see blank walls beyond them, so he knew they really were back in the bland, featureless time-hollow room. But it took a moment before his eyes would focus nearer in, on Andrea.

That *was* Andrea, wasn't it? She still had those striking gray eyes and that long brown hair that shimmered in the light. And she was wearing a deerskin dress, just like the last time he'd seen her. But she didn't quite look like herself. It wasn't just that she'd lost the sadness that had always haunted her face before. She also looked . . . older.

"Jonah, thank you," she said, bending down beside him with a quiet dignity that made her seem even more mature. "Thank you for risking your life to save mine. Again."

Was now a good time for Jonah to say, *Andrea, I thought of you the whole time I was in 1611. You had to have known I'd come back for you. I missed you so much?*

No, it wasn't the right time. Andrea was still talking.

"And most of all, thank you for saving my grandfather," Andrea finished.

Jonah blinked hard, and realized that an old man with a neatly trimmed white beard was behind her.

"Your—grandfather? I did?" Jonah blurted. "But I thought he was already dead! I saw a drawing of the funeral!"

Andrea drew back.

"What?" she gasped.

"Jonah, that was in the *other* time," Katherine said warningly beside him.

"What's that young man saying?" Andrea's grandfather asked. "And I'd still like to know how he magicked all of us here. I know science and philosophy can provide rational explanations for everything, but—"

"Jonah, we'll talk later," Andrea said, standing up again and leading her grandfather to the side. "Grandfather, perhaps this is another one of those moments you should think of as a dream. Something to inspire your art, perhaps. . . ."

"We honor you," a deeper voice rumbled from behind Andrea.

"Yeah, dude, thanks," an equally deep voice added.

Jonah blinked and squinted all over again. His eyesight was clearing up, but he still didn't quite trust it. The boys who had spoken were so tall—he should probably be thinking of them as men. But how could that be possible?

"Whoa," Katherine said beside him, catching her breath. "Brendan, is that you? And—Antonio?"

"No—it's One Who Survives Much and Walks With Pride," Antonio corrected.

"It's been a long time since anyone has called us those other names," Brendan said apologetically. "We almost forgot them."

Jonah was still blinking and trying to see the Brendan and Antonio he'd known in the giants who stood before him. They were teenage boys—it was possible for them to have grown a lot in a short time, wasn't it? Didn't Jonah's own dad always brag about how he'd grown three inches the summer he was fifteen?

Brendan and Antonio looked as if they were each more than a foot taller.

"I know this is a lot to ask, but . . . you didn't happen to save any of our artwork, did you?" Brendan asked.

"I didn't, but I saw someone else taking some big carving away," Jonah said.

Brendan and Antonio high-fived each other. It was a very high high-five.

"Then I honor art-stealing, law-breaking time travelers too!" Antonio crowed. "As long as our work survives!"

A strange look came over his face.

"JB, the plain walls in this room are killing me," he said, calling back over his shoulder. "And I've got some ideas. Okay if I do something about them?"

"The walls are the least of my worries right now," JB's voice came from the midst of a crowd of Native Americans. "Be my guest."

Jonah was relieved to see that JB was alive—and conscious.

"Mind if I borrow your shoes?" Antonio asked Jonah.

"My—shoes?" Jonah asked.

"Sure. I'll give them back in a few minutes," Antonio said.

Jonah kicked them off and watched as Antonio carried them to the wall and began pressing the soles against it. Ashy copies of the Nike imprint from the bottom of Jonah's shoes transferred to the blank wall.

Brendan produced a charred stick from somewhere and began drawing a path alongside the shoe prints.

Both of them seemed to have forgotten about Jonah and Katherine.

"Well, they're happy," Katherine muttered. "But—how old do you think they are?"

Jonah shrugged.

"Chip and Alex aged two years when we were apart from them back in the 1400s," he said. "But then they went back to normal when we went home. So does it really matter?"

"I guess not," Katherine said. But she didn't look particularly comforted.

A sheepdog wormed its way out of the crowd and rubbed against Jonah's leg.

"Dare made it out too!" Katherine rejoiced.

"Guess the Elucidator counted him as part of 'everybody' in whatever hut he was in," Jonah muttered. He patted Dare's head, but couldn't quite focus. Was there something else Jonah should be paying attention to?

He looked back at JB, who was surrounded by dozens of puzzled-looking Native Americans. They all seemed to be talking at once. JB was nodding and saying, "Um-hm, um-hm," even as he expertly swiped his fingers again and again across the screen of an Elucidator—

the Elucidator Jonah himself had been holding when he came into the time hollow.

Puzzled natives. JB. Elucidator.

Jonah struggled to get up, and then to dive toward JB and the Elucidator.

"JB, no!" Jonah screamed. "Don't just send them right back into the fire!"

JB looked up from the Elucidator.

"You think I would do that?" he asked in an offended voice.

"Because time—we changed it—you like things to be authentic—" Jonah couldn't get the words out.

"Jonah, these people have been my friends and neighbors for the past five years," JB said. "They took me in. They kept me alive. They're—they're *blood*."

One of the natives said something in Algonquin, and JB translated his own words. The native nodded vehemently, evidently agreeing about the whole "blood" relationship.

Jonah just gaped at them.

"Did you say . . . five years?" Katherine asked faintly. "You . . . and Brendan . . . and Antonio . . . and Andrea . . . were really in 1600 for five years?"

"Well, 1600 for a half year, and then 1601 for a year, and so on, until now it's 1605," JB said. "Er, that's what it was when you rescued us."

Jonah was having a hard time absorbing this.

"Then Brendan and Antonio and Andrea are all eighteen now," Jonah said, looking at the others.

"And Jonah and I are still, like, little kids," Katherine said. She was practically pouting.

Jonah almost said, *Speak for yourself*, because he didn't want Andrea thinking of him as little. But it was hopeless. She was *eighteen* now, and he was still just thirteen.

The native man beside JB said something again, and JB answered him in Algonquin: "I am sorry, honored chief, but I cannot explain everything we are discussing right now. It is a very long story, best suited for a night of talking around the campfire."

"And there is no night in this room," the native chief said, nodding. He looked around at the windowless walls. "And no day, either."

Jonah thought the chief had figured out the time hollow with incredible speed.

"So what are you going to do with everyone?" Jonah asked.

"Right now I'm just trying to figure out who is here, what happened, what's going on with time—I can't even begin to think about what we should do next," JB said. He started to look back at the Elucidator, then looked up quickly. "Except—*nobody* is going to be sent back to a certain death."

"Excuse me," a strange voice spoke from the back of the room. It sounded oddly familiar, but Jonah couldn't quite place it.

Then a boy shoved his way through the crowd toward JB and Katherine and Jonah. Was he someone Jonah had seen before? With his light hair and blue eyes, he looked out of place in the roomful of Native Americans.

"*Another* hottie?" Jonah heard Katherine murmur under her breath. "I mean, he's no Brendan or Antonio"— she glanced toward the two tall boys, who were still completely fixated on their drawings—"but, whoa."

Jonah remembered that Brendan and Antonio had said their tribe was very generous about taking in people from other cultures. He guessed that that must have happened with this boy—except that as the boy stepped closer, Jonah saw that he had the perfect straight teeth that came only from years of wearing braces. And, while all the other males in the room—even JB—were wearing some variation of loincloths or deerskin pants, this boy was wearing a Cincinnati Reds T-shirt and shorts with a little Reebok logo at the bottom.

"Can someone please tell me what's going on?" the

boy asked, his voice trembling slightly. "This guy shows up, he tells me it's my turn to go back in time, and suddenly I'm in this hut that's on fire. And then the next instant I'm in this room. What happened? Was that all I had to do? Can I go home now?"

Jonah realized that this must be one of the other missing kids from time. He would have been in the time cave back at the beginning with everyone else—that had to be the reason he seemed vaguely familiar.

JB squinted at the boy.

"What's your name, son?" JB asked, in an unusually gentle voice.

"Um." For some reason, the boy was screwing up his face and squinting at JB, as if JB had asked a difficult question. "My real name—well, *I* still think of it as my real name—I'm Dalton Sullivan."

Yep, Jonah thought. That had been the name of one of the other kids in the time cave back at the adoption conference where they'd all met. Jonah had heard the organizers call out the name Dalton Sullivan. But he'd been too preoccupied to notice or remember the boy who answered to it.

"And did anyone tell you what your original identity was?" JB asked, still speaking gently. "Or what year you were supposed to go to?"

For some reason JB practically seemed to be holding his breath.

The boy grimaced.

"Not the year part," he said, shaking his head. "But I think I'm supposed to be someone called John Hudson?"

FORTY-SEVEN

"That *hottie* was supposed to be hideous in original time?" Katherine burst out, so surprised that she didn't manage to keep her voice down.

"Um—hideous?" Dalton Sullivan/John Hudson asked, his voice trembling again. "Was there—I mean—*is* there something awful that's supposed to happen to me?"

"She just means you would have looked a little . . . uh . . . weather-beaten in 1611," Jonah said. He felt kind of defensive about the original John Hudson's appearance. "Just from the scurvy and the frostbite and the knife fights and—oh, don't worry about it. You were a pretty nice kid, no matter what you looked like. And I think you missed all the awful stuff. Right, JB?"

JB was hunched over the Elucidator, mumbling and swiping and typing in a frantic blur of motion.

"So Second sent John Hudson to 1605 instead of 1611," JB muttered. "By mistake? On purpose? What could he have been planning?" He looked directly at Dalton for a moment. "You really arrived in 1605 in the middle of the fire? You didn't go anywhere else?"

"You mean, in time?" Dalton said. "See, I think of 'going places' as being a geographical thing. This whole time-travel thing, I'm still trying to figure it out—"

"He hasn't spent more than two minutes in the past," Katherine interrupted, sounding sure of herself once more. "If he had, he wouldn't talk like that."

"But—1605?" JB repeated. "That's impossible. The original John Hudson was already *in* 1605, living in England, I'd guess. . . ." He studied the Elucidator. "Yes, absolutely. Here's the proof."

He tapped the screen.

"So, then, for about two minutes in 1605 there were two John Hudsons in the world?" Jonah asked. "I thought that was impossible unless time's unraveling. So Second was unraveling time *backward*? All the way back to 1605?"

"Yes, yes . . . ," JB said, his face awash with horror.

"Then when will it stop?" Dalton whimpered.

"Now," a voice said authoritatively.

Jonah looked around. Was the *room* speaking?

"Embedded speakers—don't anybody freak out," the walls spoke.

"Second," JB said calmly. "We meet again."

Jonah saw that Andrea's grandfather and a few of the more elderly Native Americans had fainted.

"Everybody—chill out. That's just a weird kind of thunder," Antonio said over his shoulder as he drew.

The natives stopped looking so worried.

Jonah didn't feel particularly soothed.

"Did you say we meet again?" Second's voice boomed out. "Not so much with the meeting thing. If you think through the possibilities, I'm sure you will realize that this message was prerecorded, like so many others. In fact if you've triggered this message, we shall never meet again."

"I'm sure you'll understand that I wouldn't be too upset about that—if I really believed you," JB said wryly.

"I'm downloading proof to your Elucidator right now," Second said, and the voice seemed to surround them. Everyone was cringing away from it now.

"I made a deal with Jonah and Katherine," Second continued. "They upheld their end of the bargain and saved 1611 for me. And so now I shall uphold my end of the bargain and allow them to save their friends."

"We *already* saved JB and Andrea and Brendan and Antonio, you idiot," Katherine yelled at the wall. "We did it ourselves—or, well, Jonah did. We don't need your deal anymore."

"Yes, you do," Second said, as if he could really hear her, could really answer. "If I wanted to, I could go on meddling in your time. But I promise from here on out I will stay only in mine."

"What's this 'your time, my time' you're talking about?" JB asked, looking up from the Elucidator. "Time is time is time. It's all interconnected. Even if you stay in 1611, everything you do will affect the future. And these kids' lives are uniquely at risk if—"

"You still don't get it, do you?" Second thundered. "Poor JB, you're such a rule follower, you can't even think about what's possible if the rules are broken. I'll walk you through this one. We've always known time protects itself, right? So if someone throws too many changes at time, creates too many paradoxes—"

"Time collapses," JB said grimly. Under the ash and soot on his face he'd gone pale.

"Usually," Second agreed. "But not if the paradoxes are carefully controlled. It's like how twentieth-century scientists figured out that splitting the atom wasn't just useful for creating incredibly destructive bombs. They could also use nuclear energy to power lightbulbs."

"But—think about Three Mile Island," JB muttered.

"Chernobyl. People make mistakes. It's too dangerous to—"

"Ah, but Jonah and Katherine protected everyone from any mistakes I might have made, splitting time," Second said confidently. "They fixed everything."

"We did?" Jonah asked, startled.

He remembered the moment in the shallop when everything had seemed to divide: one shallop full of sailors headed toward shore, the other going back to a ship that appeared out of nowhere. Time *had* split in that moment. One version was healed, and the tracers came back.

The other version was changed—and completely under Second's control.

"I was confident that Jonah and Katherine would choose to save people—Wydowse, in the shallop, and their friends in 1605," Second explained. "They're very predictable."

"Did you predict just how *many* people Jonah would save from 1605?" JB muttered. He looked around at the roomful of people. Then he caught Jonah's eye. "Not that I'm complaining. I would not wish to be mourning my friends right now."

JB slung his arm around the chief's shoulder. The chief had been staring at the talking walls in befuddlement, but now he looked at JB and nodded stoutly.

Jonah looked at Katherine.

"Second did kill Wydowse in that other version of

time," Jonah said. He was certain of it now. "He'll probably kill other people, too. He doesn't care."

"Why should I?" Second answered. "These people already get their regular lives, in original time. Aren't I being generous, giving them a second chance at life anyway? Giving them other choices?"

"You don't give chances or choices," Jonah said. "You just force people to do what you want!"

Jonah didn't feel like he was talking to a wall, talking back to a recording. Even though he knew Second wasn't there for real, Jonah felt like he was finally getting to tell him off.

It felt really good.

For a long moment the wall was silent. Jonah thought maybe he'd won the argument. Maybe Second was completely done talking.

Then Second whispered back.

"Oh, Jonah, haven't you been making your own choices all along?" Second asked. "What choice do you want that you don't have?"

"The choice to . . . ," Jonah began, and then he stopped. This felt dangerous, like telling a genie your wishes in a fairy tale. What if it really mattered what he said?

He thought about what he'd wanted so badly ever since he'd landed on the deck of Henry Hudson's ship.

Fix time, save Andrea, save everyone else . . . Now that he and Katherine had accomplished those things, anything else he might ask for seemed childish and silly.

I want Andrea to be my girlfriend. Well that wasn't going to work out if she was eighteen and he was thirteen. And, anyhow that would have to be her choice, too.

I want all the natives and John White and even Dare to be taken care of, to have good lives, and the people back in 1611 to be okay.

Again, that wasn't really something he could control.

I want a million dollars, I want a TV and a computer in my room at home, I want all the kids at school to like me, I want to just be Jonah Skidmore and not have to be anybody else anywhere else or anytime else. . . .

He realized that everyone was watching him, waiting for his answer. And he realized what he wanted most.

"I just want to go home," he said. "Me and Katherine— we've been away a long time."

"But of course." Second's voice poured from the walls. "Of course you want to go home. Don't you know this is all over now, and you can?"

That's prerecorded, Jonah reminded himself. *Once again Second knew exactly what I was going to say.*

But he couldn't worry about that right now. Because JB was nodding, agreeing with Second. And then Katherine was grabbing Jonah and hugging him and jumping up and down, all at the same time.

"We're going home!" she shrieked.

"We're going home," Jonah repeated, almost too dazed to believe it. "We get to go home."

EPILOGUE

Jonah stood in front of the open refrigerator.

"Turkey, ham, pepperoni, Swiss cheese, cheddar cheese, lettuce, tomato, mayonnaise, mustard . . . ," he muttered as he grabbed each item.

"Jonah, what are you doing?" his mother asked behind him. "You just had breakfast an hour ago."

Jonah shrugged.

"I'm hungry again," he said. "Any sourdough bread left?"

"Yes—er, no. Katherine finished it yesterday. Have the whole wheat." Mom handed it to him. "How could you both be having such massive growth spurts at the same time?" she asked.

Jonah decided not to tell his mother the real reason he and Katherine were eating like starving people—because they *had* been starving. It'd been a week since they'd arrived home from their time travels, and Jonah still felt as if he needed to make up for all the calories he'd missed in 1600 and 1611.

Now Jonah had all the food he wanted, but he still stood in front of the refrigerator admiring everything that was available to him: the full gallon jug of milk, the brightly colored carton of orange juice, the Tupperware container of beef stew left over from last night . . .

Hmm. Maybe that would be good with my sandwich, he thought. *Or maybe as another snack in an hour or so.*

"Jonah?" Mom said. "If you're going to be doubling our grocery bills, could you at least try to keep the electricity bill down?"

"Huh?" Jonah said.

"Shut the refrigerator!" Mom said. But she didn't sound mad. Just puzzled. She kept watching Jonah as he jumped back and shoved the door forward. "People warned me the teen years would be interesting," she muttered, mostly to herself.

Jonah assembled his sandwich as quickly as he could, and took it outside to eat. He didn't want Mom noticing anything else. It wasn't as if he thought Mom would actually figure out on her own, *Oh, yeah! Jonah and Katherine have been flitting in and out of various life-threatening situations in history!*

That's *why they're acting weird!* But she seemed to know that something was going on.

And Jonah still didn't quite trust himself not to throw his arms around his mother and cry out, "Thank you for having food in the house! Thank you for not making me hunt for it myself! And thank you for not sending me off to be a ship's boy with a bunch of mean sailors when I was a little kid!"

This past week he'd been even more tempted to tell too much to his dad. On Tuesday night, when Dad was helping Jonah with his math homework, Jonah had come very close to slipping and saying, "Dad, I'm really glad *you* didn't want your name written on the tablets of the sea! You may not go down in history, but I'd rather have you as my dad than crazy old Henry Hudson!"

Maybe Jonah just needed to avoid both his parents for a little while. At least he could still talk to Katherine.

As soon as Jonah stepped out onto the front porch, Katherine yelled over to him from the driveway.

"Want to play basketball?" she asked. "We were just getting started."

She was with their friend Chip. The last time the three of them had played basketball in the driveway—along with another friend, Alex—JB had shown up and whisked the two siblings off to the 1600s. As far as Chip or Alex could tell, on that Saturday afternoon a week ago, no time at all had passed before Jonah and Katherine were back again.

"I think time travel has kind of ruined basketball for me," Jonah said now, trying to keep his voice even. "Want to walk over to the park and see if anyone's got a game of soccer going?"

"No, thanks," Katherine said.

Jonah looked to Chip, then realized that Katherine had spoken for him, too. Jonah and Chip had been friends before Chip and Katherine had become boyfriend-girlfriend, but suddenly Jonah felt like an outsider in his own front yard.

A third wheel.

"Okay," Jonah said. "See you later."

He went into the garage to grab a soccer ball as he gobbled down his sandwich. He yelled into the house to let Mom know where he was going.

"Take your cell phone!" Mom called after him.

Jonah wished he could see how she'd react if he said, *You know, Katherine and I were roaming around a remote area of old-timey Canada without a cell phone or a working Elucidator, and we had to deal with a crazy guy who didn't care who lived or died—and we did just fine. Do you really think it's going to be that dangerous for me, just walking over to the park?*

Actually, he probably didn't want to see how she'd react to that. What if she believed him?

Jonah kicked at dead leaves on the sidewalk as he headed toward the park. It was the second week of November, but still warmer than June had been in James Bay back in 1611. Several of his neighbors were out in their yards raking leaves, reseeding their grass, or planting flower bulbs that would bloom in the spring.

All this could have been different, Jonah thought. *Or—all this could have ceased to exist.*

Was that still possible?

Jonah decided he'd concentrate on kicking the soccer ball along the sidewalk, rather than thinking about the fate of the world. He went five blocks without losing control of the ball. Then he had to give it an extra-hard kick to cross Albans Street.

A man bent over to scoop up the ball on the opposite corner. When he stood up, Jonah saw who it was: JB.

Jonah felt like turning around and running back to his house. And then maybe going up to his room and locking the door and climbing into bed and pulling the covers over his face.

"I'm not ready," Jonah said. "If you're here to send me on another trip through time—"

JB held up his hands like he was surrendering.

"No one's ready," JB said. "No more trips through time for a while. I promise."

He tossed the ball back to Jonah. Jonah caught it and finished crossing the street.

"Then why are you here?" Jonah asked. The words were out of his mouth before he realized how rude they sounded. "I mean—"

"I know what you mean," JB said. "I came to walk to the park with you."

He began heading on down Albans.

"You know, it's really creepy that you know where I'm going," Jonah objected.

"Soccer ball, soccer fields," JB said, pointing first to the ball Jonah was carrying, then toward the park just around the next corner. "It was a deduction, not any time-travel spying."

"Oh," Jonah said. He caught up with JB.

"I thought I'd let you and Katherine know how things stand with Second's little, uh, time experiment," JB said. "But when I checked in at your house, it looked like Katherine was busy."

"Ugh," Jonah said, making a disgusted face. "Don't remind me."

"She and Chip are only playing basketball," JB said, looking down at the screen of something that appeared to be an iPhone but was probably his Elucidator. "Though it seems like an unusually *friendly* competition."

Jonah rolled his eyes.

"Have the time police caught up with Second yet?" he asked, ready to change the subject.

"No," JB said. "And unless we make some massive advance in our understanding of time travel, they never will. He's sealed off his new version of time so well that no one can get to him."

Jonah thought about the duplicated versions of the crew members on the *Discovery*, sailing along Second's made-up Northwest Passage. Would Staffe be all right? Would Henry Hudson? What would any of them think when they found nothing left of John Hudson but his cape?

"Katherine and I should have stopped Second when we had the chance," Jonah said.

"No, you did exactly what you needed to do," JB said. "You really did save all of time. Not that you'll ever be able to put that on your—what's that thing that's really important for kids in your time period? Oh, yeah—college applications. It's a shame you won't be able to put any of this on your college applications."

"College is a long way away," Jonah mumbled, slightly embarrassed by the admiration shining in JB's eyes.

"Besides, it's not like me and Katherine really deserve that much credit. We just did what Second expected us to do."

"No," JB said, shaking his head fiercely. "You deserve a lot of credit. Second just thought he knew what you would do—he thought it'd bother you that he was so blatant, sailing the ship from the wrong direction. He thought the more he tried to distract you from Wydowse's death, the more you'd focus on it. And—"

"That's what I mean," Jonah muttered. "Second manipulated us the whole time."

JB's head-shaking became even more vehement.

"Second could only manipulate the circumstances," JB said. "It was still you and Katherine making your own choices. You still had free will. So the world owes you for caring about Wydowse, for caring about me and Brendan and Antonio and Andrea—and for caring about all the natives in the burning village. If you hadn't started saving everyone, John Hudson would have perished too."

"And that would have been enough to mess up time forever?" Jonah asked.

"Yes," JB said grimly. "Can you see why we're suspending time travel for a while?"

Jonah almost dropped his soccer ball.

"Wait—you mean, it's not just my trip back to my . . . my other identity that's being postponed?" Jonah asked.

"No," JB said. "It's all trips before the twenty-first century. What you heard me say when you first got to 1611, about how many mistakes we made—that's all true. Second's escapades pointed out dozens of misconceptions we still need to overcome. We have to make sure we're not going to make an even bigger mess of things before we go back to replacing missing children in time."

Jonah felt a wave of relief. Maybe he could even live out his whole life before JB got around to coming back for him. Maybe it would never matter again that Jonah belonged in a different time and place.

"Yeah, you know, time travel—what's it really good for if I could save the whole world and not even get a girl-friend out of it?" Jonah asked, the relief making him a little giddy.

"Jonah, about Andrea—," JB began.

"Forget I said anything," Jonah said, suddenly embar-rassed.

"No, you have to understand—the poor girl's been through a lot," JB said. "It's nothing personal against you."

"Yeah, yeah," Jonah said. "Whatever."

"Jonah, you—oh!" JB stared down at his Elucidator in surprise. "It appears that Andrea is on her way here right now, to talk to you. She just stopped at your house, and Katherine told her where to find you."

"Something else to be annoyed with Katherine about," Jonah muttered.

But when Andrea showed up a few minutes later with a woman in a white Honda, Jonah couldn't help being happy to see her.

She didn't look like she was eighteen anymore. When she got out of the passenger side of the car, she stood shorter than Jonah once again.

"Aunt Patty, I kind of need to talk to Jonah privately," she called back to the woman in the car.

"That's fine," the woman said patiently.

"Want to go sit on those swings?" Andrea asked, pointing across the park.

"Sure," Jonah said.

He saw that JB leaned in to talk to Andrea's aunt while they waited. Jonah wondered what JB could possibly find to say without bringing up some touchy topic: *Hey, sorry about kidnapping your niece and taking her four hundred years back in time. Sorry she got stuck there for five years. Sorry we had to count on a thirteen-year-old to rescue her. Oh, wait—you don't know about any of that, do you?*

Then Jonah and Andrea reached the swings, and Jonah couldn't think of anything safe to talk about with her, either.

"Have you seen Brendan and Antonio since we got back?" Andrea asked.

"No," Jonah said. "I tried to call Brendan once, but his mom said he was busy painting."

"It's a good thing they've got their art," Andrea said. "That's how they're dealing with all of this. Let me tell you, they're both furious at having to live through being thirteen all over again."

"What about you?" Jonah said. He didn't quite dare to look at her.

"I'm looking at it as another chance," Andrea said. "There are things I didn't see before. . . . I was really mean to Aunt Patty and Uncle Rob, and I shouldn't have been. They're almost as sad as I am about my parents dying. And now I've had five years of dealing with the grief that they haven't had yet. So it's like it's my job now to comfort them."

"That's weird," Jonah said. He sat down in one of the swings and pushed off, letting the momentum carry him back and forth.

Andrea giggled.

"They think my 'new mature attitude' is all because I signed up for an adopt-a-grandparent program at a local nursing home," she said. "And I've hit it off with a slightly senile old man who has the delusion that he's from the past."

"JB let your real grandfather come to the twenty-first century?" Jonah asked in amazement.

Andrea nodded. "*And* JB relocated all the Native Americans from the village to a nature preserve in the future," she said.

"JB's gone soft," Jonah said. "He cares about a lot more besides time now."

"Yeah," Andrea said. "It's hard to know where this is all going to end."

She sat down in the swing beside Jonah's and turned toward him.

"I'm sorry," she said.

"That JB's gone soft?" Jonah asked.

"No—that we're not going to be girlfriend-boyfriend like Katherine and Chip are girlfriend-boyfriend," Andrea said.

Jonah almost fell out of the swing.

"I'm not Second," he said. "*I* wouldn't want to go around manipulating people into doing things they don't want to do."

"It's not that," Andrea said. "It's just that there's so much else to deal with. I was eighteen, now I'm thirteen. I was Virginia Dare, now I'm Andrea Crowell again. I was used to living in the woods and cooking over an open flame and owning exactly one outfit—and now I've got to remember how to use my iPod and computer again. And don't get me started on how hard it is to remember if

Hollister clothes are cooler than Abercrombie and Fitch, or if it's the other way around. Everything's just too weird right now for me to think about anything else."

This was practically the longest string of sentences Jonah had ever heard Andrea say.

"My mom acts like life is supposed to be weird when you're a teenager," Jonah said. He grinned. "But I don't think any of this was what she was talking about."

"Jonah . . . even if we can't be boyfriend-girlfriend . . . we can still be two kids who know how to deal with weird things together," Andrea said.

Strangely, this seemed like one of the nicest things anyone had ever said to Jonah.

"That sounds good," he said, trying hard to make his voice sound light and carefree.

He still thought Andrea understood.

They sat in silence for a few moments, until Andrea's aunt gave a brief beep of her horn.

"I've got to go," Andrea said. She surprised him by giving him a quick hug. "But I'll call, or text, or IM, or . . ."

She was already across the park and climbing into the car with her aunt before she'd finished listing ways they could communicate.

Just because she doesn't want to be my girlfriend now, that doesn't mean she won't want to be my girlfriend in the future, Jonah thought.

JB came walking toward him as soon as Andrea and her aunt drove off.

"You look happier," JB observed.

"Why not?" Jonah said. "I don't have scurvy. I don't have frostbite. I'm not in the middle of a mutiny. Nobody's threatening me with a knife or a gun or a sword. Katherine and I got out of 1611. Time didn't collapse. Everyone got out of 1605. And Andrea didn't say she would *never* be my girlfriend." He took a deep breath. "The future looks pretty bright, don't you think?"

"It's good that you can think so," JB said, smiling indulgently.

Should I worry that he didn't completely agree? Jonah wondered. But Jonah had done enough worrying in the 1600s to last him for a lifetime. If there was something bad waiting for him in the future—or the past—he didn't want to know about it now. Not when the sun was shining and his stomach was full and he wouldn't have to go back in time again anytime soon.

"Hey, Jonah!" someone yelled from across the park. For the first time Jonah noticed that a group of kids from school were playing soccer at the opposite end of the park. They were too far away for Jonah even to see who was calling to him. "Want to play?"

Jonah looked at JB.

"Go on," JB said, giving him a little shove on the back. "Have fun."

JB turned away. He probably thought that Jonah was going to race off to the game immediately. But Jonah didn't. He stood there a moment longer, and so he heard the rest of what JB said: "Have fun . . . while you still can."

AUTHOR'S NOTE

I can't tell you what happened to the real John Hudson in real history.

This probably doesn't surprise you if you've read the author's notes at the back of previous books in the Missing series. Like Virginia Dare (from *Sabotaged*) and Edward V and his brother, Richard (from *Sent*), John Hudson truly is one of the missing children in history.

However, John Hudson's situation is a little stranger than the other kids'. It's not just that he and his father vanished from history. It's that the stories about the last moments before they vanished sound so much like lies.

John Hudson was ship's boy for all four of his father's known voyages. He was probably about twelve to fourteen at the time of the first voyage in 1607, which would have made him sixteen to eighteen at the time of the mutiny on the *Discovery*. As ship's boy he probably would have been expected to run errands, stand watch, deliver messages, repair ropes, swab the deck, help the ship's cook, and follow whatever other orders he was given. Since he was not just ship's boy but also the captain's son, it's easy to believe that part of John's duties might have been learning how to lead a ship of his own someday.

If that's the case, his father provided a rather mixed role model.

Like numerous European explorers before and after him, Henry Hudson was eager to find a better route to the rich trade goods of China and India and other places in Asia. In 1607 and 1608 he tried going northeast from England, encountering crippling ice each time. He did manage to sail closer to the North Pole than any European ship's captain before him—and his travels proved once and for all that the polar areas would not be as warm as the tropics in the summertime, even with all the sunlight.

In 1609 Hudson sailed on behalf of a Dutch company, rather than the English. Although he swore on a Bible that he would go back and keep searching in a northeasterly direction, by now Henry Hudson was more interested in looking for a route to the northwest—through or above North America. He first sailed to the northeast, then broke his promise and headed west. This voyage became his most famous one, as it led to his discovery of the Hudson River and gave the Dutch a basis for claiming the lands of New Netherland (part of present-day New York and nearby areas).

And as a result of that voyage, Hudson was viewed as a traitor in England. Hudson feared that King James would have him thrown into prison for making such a huge discovery for another country. But English investors seemed to decide, *Hey, if he can do that for the Dutch— what can he do for us?* And so they funded a voyage for Hudson to look for the Northwest Passage under the English flag.

By the time of Hudson's fourth voyage he'd established himself as an able sailor. Three times he'd sailed into dangerous icy waters in ships that were hardly suited to Arctic conditions. And three times he'd managed to return home safely—two of those times without losing a single man from his crew.

However, the records of Hudson's first three voyages show numerous occasions where he wasn't nearly as good at dealing with people as he was at sailing. Part of the problem might have been that frightened, cooped-up sailors in desperate situations aren't exactly the easiest people to manage. But it appears that his crews were near mutiny more than once.

This pattern was to continue on the fourth voyage.

The *Discovery*, with a crew of twenty-three—including John Hudson and another ship's boy, Nicholas Symmes—sailed from London on April 17, 1610. The intrigue began almost immediately, as Hudson stopped by Gravesend, England, five days later to let off one crew member he'd decided to dismiss, and to pick up another crew member, Henry Greene, who was widely considered to be a troublemaker.

And Greene was to become heavily involved in the troubles on the *Discovery*.

Hudson sailed around the tip of Greenland and then headed farther north than he'd gone on his previous trip to North America. He crossed the Davis Strait and sailed into what was then known as the Furious Overfall—the entry to what would become the Hudson Strait. Struggling through ice and dangerous currents, the *Discovery* entered the Hudson Bay and sailed south. Some of the names Hudson gave to the lands he found along the way may have indicated his state of mind: Desire Provoketh, Isles of God's Mercies, Hold with Hope.

The account Hudson kept of his voyage on the *Discovery* ended on August 3, 1610, more than ten months before the mutiny. It is likely that Hudson actually wrote a longer account, but the mutineers may have destroyed it because it made them look even guiltier. What survives of Hudson's account is fairly dry and factual, dealing mostly with latitude readings and weather reports.

It fell to others to describe the arguments and anger that simmered on the ship.

The longest report from the voyage was written by the bizarrely named Abacuk Prickett—yes, there really was a person with that name. Before joining the crew of the *Discovery*, he had worked as a London haberdasher and as a servant of one of the investors in the expedition. This would not be the most likely career path toward becoming a sailor.

According to Prickett, about a month and a half into the journey some of the crew got mad when Henry Greene started a fistfight with another man and Hudson took Greene's side. Soon after, first mate Robert Juet began spreading rumors that Greene was a spy for Hudson. And, not long after that, Hudson demoted Juet and held a trial for him that might have left Juet believing he would be hanged when he returned to England. Later Greene himself got mad at Hudson when another crew member died and Hudson gave the man's coat to Greene, but then took it back and let someone else have it instead. This is just one of several times Prickett claims Hudson reversed his decisions or waffled back and forth, infuriating everyone.

Thomas Wydowse—who was indeed one of the sickly men sent out in the shallop—really did leave behind at least one note about the tensions on the ship. He was a mathematician, on the voyage to help with navigation, and so was better educated than others in the crew. (Especially considering that many of the men could neither read nor write.) Wydowse's writings, found in his desk when the *Discovery* returned to England, also tell of the accusations and trial against Juet in September 1610.

Even as the tensions grew among the crew, the *Discovery* was sailing farther and farther south, deeper and deeper into the Hudson Bay. Hudson undoubtedly hoped that they would reach a more temperate region before winter hit—perhaps even the South Seas.

Instead he was sailing into a dead end.

If you look at a map of Canada, you can see instantly what a huge cutout the Hudson Bay makes in the land. Hudson and his men sailed all the way to the bottom of it, into the slightly narrower James Bay.

By late October it was more than clear that they wouldn't make it back to England before winter hit, as Hudson had done on his three previous trips. And the icy waters around them certainly looked nothing like the South Seas. If they tried to keep sailing, they faced numerous dangers. One was that the ice might completely trap them. They also faced the risk of having the ship smashed to bits by the huge ice floes churning around them.

Hudson apparently chose to ground his ship in the safest area he could find, away from the worst of the ice. According to Prickett, Hudson ordered Philip Staffe, the ship's carpenter, to build a winter cabin on the nearby land. In what seems to have been an uncharacteristic act of defiance, Staffe refused, saying, essentially, *I'm a ship's carpenter. I don't do houses.* But he apparently relented soon afterward, and did build a shelter. Prickett said that building the house took "much labor" but was "of little use."

Winters along James Bay are brutal, with temperatures falling as low as forty or fifty degrees below zero. And Hudson's men had no North Face fleece, no microfiber, no Under Armour. In fact, the warmest clothes they had probably would have been made of wool. If they got their clothes wet, it would have been like asking for frostbite.

According to Prickett, the cold weather "lamed most of the crew."

Surprisingly, though, during the first part of the winter they felt quite blessed with their food supplies. Prickett wrote that partridges were so plentiful nearby that "we killed more than a hundred dozen," along with other kinds of birds, and "we had all the fish we could net."

Then, as spring approached, the flocks of partridges

flew away, and soon the other birds did as well. The fish evidently became more difficult to catch too. Prickett said the men were reduced to foraging through "the woods and hills and valleys in search of anything that had any substance to it, no matter how vile: Nothing was spared, including moss of the ground, compared to which rotten wood is better, and the frog, which in breeding time is as loathsome as the toad."

It wasn't just that this minimal food tasted awful—it also failed to provide basic nutrients. No one in 1611 completely understood the link between certain foods and certain diseases, but they'd figured out a little bit. Prickett mentioned that Thomas Wydowse brewed a turpentine-like substance from the bud of a local tree to treat what must have been severe symptoms of scurvy.

If you remember that scurvy is what you get if you don't have enough vitamin C, then congratulations. I hope that you're never in a position to find out for yourself just what an unpleasant disease this is. People with scurvy get weaker and weaker, and they become more and more exhausted. Their gums hurt and their teeth begin to fall out. Their bones could crumble. They faint easily. They have pale skin, sunken eyes, aching muscles, internal bleeding, and, eventually, hemorrhaging. New wounds take longer to heal; old wounds, such as sword cuts that might have healed years earlier, can reopen.

Sounds fun, doesn't it? If this has made you want to go get a big glass of orange juice to drink while you're reading this, that's fine with me. Just drink it fast, because I'm going to be talking about some really disgusting food in a little bit.

Amazingly, in spite of the terrible cold and the lack of food and the widespread ailments, all but one man survived the winter. As the ice broke up in the bay and everyone prepared to sail again, food stores were so low that Hudson decided to divide up the only bread and cheese they had left. Each crew member got a supply meant to last fourteen days—even though Hudson was warned that some of the men would just gobble up their share immediately and then not have anything. And this was exactly what happened. One man even ate so much bread in one day that he made himself sick. Others began to whisper that Hudson was actually hiding food, keeping the best for himself and his favorites. Hudson, meanwhile, thought his men were stealing food, so he had ship's boy Nicholas Symmes search all their sea chests. This made the men even madder.

On top of all the worries and disputes about food, when they began sailing again, Hudson did not rush immediately northeast, toward home and food and safety.

Instead he went back to sailing northwest.

How could he still be looking for the Northwest Passage while his men were so close to starving?

On June 18, 1610, the *Discovery* got trapped in ice once more, and Hudson could not sail in any direction. Three days later, when the ice finally broke up, the resentments and fears boiled over—into mutiny.

In previous books in this series I have been very careful not to change any historical details—I've just filled in the gaps in the historical record with some very weird fictionalized possibilities. In this book I did not feel so strongly that I needed to stick precisely to the historical record. Partly that's because Second has messed up time so completely in my version of the tale.

But the stories that Prickett and his fellow survivors told about the mutiny sound pretty messed up too.

Messed up as in—how could anybody have believed them?

Prickett began his account of the actual mutiny by telling how two of the mutineers—Henry Greene and William Wilson—came to him the night before and told what they planned to do. Prickett was "lying lame in [his] cabin," which provided an excuse for not going to warn the captain. But he said he told Wilson and Greene that mutiny was evil, and that he begged them not to do it. One after another, other mutineers came to talk to Prickett that night. Thinking it might help, he said he got each man to swear an oath that they would not actually harm any man, and that what they were doing was for the good of the voyage.

Later Prickett concluded that the purpose of the oath had actually backfired—it made each man determined to carry out the rebellion.

According to Prickett, as soon as Hudson came out of his cabin the next morning, two men cornered him and a third bound his arms behind him. Down in the hold the loyal John King really did take a sword and go on the attack in Hudson's defense, but he was outnumbered and subdued. The mutineers took him up on the deck with Hudson.

After that, Prickett said, the mutineers brought up the shallop to the ship's side and put the "poor, sick, and lame men" into it. Prickett's account never explains how he could have been too lame to warn the captain the night before and yet healthy enough by morning that he wasn't put into the shallop. However, Prickett did say:

> I came out of my cabin as best I could
> to speak to the master at the hatchway
> when he called me; on my knees I begged
> them [the mutineers], for the love of

God, to remember themselves and to do
onto others as they would have others
do onto them. They told me to take care,
and get back into my cabin, not allowing
the master to speak with me. But when
I returned to my cabin, he called to me
by the horn and told me that Juet would
overthrow us all; no, I said, and not softly
either, it is the villainy of Henry Greene.

Next, Prickett said, the carpenter, Staffe, decided on his own that he wanted to go with the captain in the shallop rather than stay on the ship with the mutineers. He asked only that he be given his chest "and all that's in it," and the mutineers complied.

Prickett said Staffe warned him that no one left on the ship was capable of sailing it back to England. He also said that Staffe took "a gun with powder and shot, some spears, an iron pot with some grain, and a few other things." The mutineers sailed out of the ice with the shallop attached by a rope; when they were away from the ice, they cut the shallop adrift.

Afterward, Prickett said, the mutineers did find grain, butter, pork, peas, biscuits, and a cask of beer the captain had been hoarding.

The rest of the *Discovery*'s voyage was hardly easy. According to Prickett, a tragic encounter with natives on July 28 left four men dead. And as they sailed back toward England, the only food the survivors had to live on was the bones left over from birds they'd shot previously. The crew ate the bones fried in candle wax and doused in vinegar.

One more crew member died during this crossing, probably because of starvation: Prickett said that Robert Juet "died miserably for mere want." After that the other men seemed to give up: "Some would just sit, watching the foresail or mainsail break free, the sheets either flying or broken, and not bother to do anything about it, or even call for help."

And then they caught a glimpse of land: Ireland.

Even that was not exactly the salvation they expected, as the Irish they first encountered "had neither bread, drink, nor money amongst them." Finally the crew members pawned an anchor and cable to get bread, beer, and beef, and then they were able to sail on to England.

Only eight of the original twenty-three men and boys on the *Discovery* made it back to England. They arrived in a ship with massive bloodstains on the deck— but the survivors said that was from the attack by the natives, not the mutiny. And, ever so conveniently, the survivors said that every one of the men who had truly been responsible for the mutiny had died during the rest of the voyage: Juet, Greene, and William Wilson.

Despite the dire predictions that returning to England would mean death by hanging, at first nothing happened. Prickett, Robert Bylot, and the ship's surgeon, Edward Wilson, all gave reports or depositions, and one of the agencies that had power over the shipping industry gave the opinion that hanging was in order. But nobody seemed to be in a hurry to carry it out.

Edward Wilson's account, dated January 25, 1611, differed slightly from Prickett's—he said that Staffe asked for clothes, not his chest, when he went out to the shallop. And he said that six of the men put into the shallop thought they were there only to keep Hudson and John King company while the mutineers divided up the food fairly. Wilson said those men went into the shallop "willingly, but later, when they found they were not allowed to come back on the ship again, they desired that they might have their clothes, of which a part of them were delivered."

It seems odd that the men would be so concerned about clothes, rather than food.

Edward Wilson also said that he didn't know anything about the mutiny until it was half over and he saw the master tied up. Wilson claimed, "I would have come out of my cabin to have given some food to them, but those who had bound the master told me that if I were well enough off, I should keep myself so."

Did that make him guilty too? Were all eight of the *Discovery* survivors guilty of mutiny because they hadn't gone out into the shallop with their captain?

Five more years passed before anyone decided to look closely at those questions. It's not hard to guess why justice was so slow if you know what else was going on: In 1612 at least two of the *Discovery* survivors—Robert Bylot and Abacuk Prickett—went back to Hudson Bay supported by a new company called the Discoverers of the North-west Passage.

Essentially, they must have said, *You know, if you hang us for murder, you'll never know if we really did find the secret location of the Northwest Passage. . . .*

As an afterthought they might also have promised to look for Hudson and the other abandoned men.

Bylot and Prickett and the rest of their expedition found neither the Northwest Passage nor any sign of Hudson and his men. Bylot made another search for the Northwest Passage—in Baffin Bay this time—in 1616.

Again, of course, he failed to find it.

Also in 1616 all eight *Discovery* survivors were indicted for murder. The charge was that the survivors had placed Hudson, his son, and seven others "in a certain shallop in the ice, without victuals, drink, fire, and clothing." The indictment went on to say that "by reason thereof they [the men in the shallop] came to their death and miserably did perish. And that Robert Bylot and etc. did kill and murder Henry Hudson."

Prickett, defending himself, said no one was "shot at or hurt in any way" during the mutiny. Bylot made it sound like the men in the shallop had agreed to leave on their own. Another crew member, Bennet Matthew, claimed that even after being put in the shallop, Hudson and some of the others came back onto the ship to warm up and to get some of their things—and then climbed back into the shallop.

How could all the men in the shallop have gone so peacefully? How could anyone believe the survivors' stories—especially when there were so many bloodstains covering the ship's deck?

Whether anyone believed them or not, none of the survivors ended up being hanged. Bylot was pardoned because he'd managed to sail the *Discovery* home safely with the rest of the men; Edward Wilson and Prickett were found not guilty; by 1618 charges were thrown out against everybody else who was still alive.

Maybe Prickett and the others made Hudson sound crazy enough that the mutiny seemed justifiable. Maybe after seven years had passed, no one really cared that much anymore.

Or maybe, even after multiple failed voyages, the English were still holding out hope that someone from the *Discovery* could find the elusive Northwest Passage.

It actually does exist, though not in a way that would have helped Henry Hudson even if he'd found it. If you look at a current map of North America—not one of the sketchy, half-guessed 1600s maps that Hudson would have used—you'll see a number of possible routes around and through the islands that make up northern Canada and Alaska. The maps I consulted show these waterways in pastel blue, as if the seas there are as open and clear as the Caribbean. But for most of the year those routes are iced over, and they certainly would have been impassable for a ship as primitive as the *Discovery*. The first time anyone managed to sail all the way through was in 1906, when the Norwegian explorer Roald Amundsen completed the route—after spending three winters trapped in ice.

Recently the Northwest Passage has received renewed attention because of climate change. Although climate change could certainly cause awful problems elsewhere, some point out that as more ice melts, the Northwest Passage could actually become a useful shipping route—finally achieving Hudson's dream.

But perhaps you, like Jonah and Katherine, are more concerned about the people involved than the fate of the Northwest Passage. Perhaps the burning question in your mind is not, *What good is the Northwest Passage?* but *What happened to John Hudson and the others left in a shallop in the ice?*

Truly, nobody knows for sure. But that hasn't stopped lots of people from speculating.

Since the men managed to survive the winter of 1610–1611, it's not too much of a stretch to suppose that at least some of them might have survived other winters, other years. This would have been even more likely if they were able to learn from natives in the area (who probably would have been Cree, near James Bay, rather than Inuit, as Katherine supposes). Not surprisingly, in his previous encounters with Native Americans, Hudson seemed no better at dealing with people from other cultures than he was at dealing with his own men. But maybe others in the shallop were more capable of diplomacy.

Perhaps at least some of the men in the shallop managed to keep alive on the hope that a rescue mission would come for them from England. This hope would have been overly optimistic. But two later English expeditions—one in 1631, the other in 1668–1670—each found remains of a shelter that might have been built by an English carpenter. Of course, either of these structures could have been the shelter Staffe erected in 1610 for the entire crew of the *Discovery*, so these finds don't prove anything about the men in the shallop.

A few legends told by natives might also be relevant. According to a website dedicated to Henry Hudson (www.ianchadwick.com/hudson), one of those legends tells of Inuits finding a small boat containing dead white men—and a single living boy. Could it have been John Hudson? The story ends anticlimactically: The Inuits weren't sure what to do with the boy, so they tied him outside with their dogs. It's hard to believe he would have survived that for long.

Another story told in the Ottawa Valley claims that Henry Hudson and others from the shallop—possibly including John Hudson—became slaves for natives before being killed. Supposedly they traveled down the Ottawa River, and a stone was found there reading HH CAPTIVE 1612. But the markings have never been authenticated.

Yet another theory came up more recently. Based on accounts of graves found on Spitzbergen Island off the coast of Norway, a researcher in England speculated that

Hudson and his remaining men might have managed to sail their tiny shallop three thousand miles across the Arctic before dying back in Europe, if not quite back home in England.

It sounds like an outlandish theory—but is it any more outlandish than putting eight men and a teenager out in a tiny boat in the middle of ice and just sailing away?

ACKNOWLEDGMENTS

Even though this is very much a fictionalized account of the mutiny on the *Discovery*, I am grateful to many experts who have studied and written about the true event. In particular, I appreciate the assistance I got by e-mail from Peter C. Mancall, professor of history and anthropology at the University of Southern California; director of the USC-Huntington Early Modern Studies Institute; and author of the book, *Fatal Journey: The Final Expedition of Henry Hudson*. I'm also very grateful to William "Chip" Reynolds, captain of the replica ship *Half Moon* and director of the New Netherland Museum, for answering my questions about Henry Hudson and what it would have been like to sail on one of his ships. I apologize for all the instances when—for the sake of the story—I went with less-plausible explanations than the experts gave me.

I'm also grateful to my friends Linda Gerber, Erin MacLellan, Jenny Patton, Nancy Roe Pimm, and Linda Stanek for reading portions of this book and making suggestions. And, as always, I appreciate the help from my agents, Tracey and Josh Adams; my editor, David Gale; and everyone else at Simon & Schuster who has supported this series.